THE LIONESS
IS THE HUNTER

Books by Loren D. Estleman

*Published by Tom Doherty Associates

THE LIONESS IS THE HUNTER

An Amos Walker Novel

Loren D. Estleman

A Tom Doherty Associates Book
New York

This is a work of fiction. All of the characters, organizations, and events portrayed in this novel are either products of the author's imagination or are used fictitiously.

A Forge Book
Published by Tom Doherty Associates
175 Fifth Avenue
New York, NY 10010

www.tor-forge.com

Forge® is a registered trademark of Macmillan Publishing Group, LLC.

The Library of Congress Cataloging-in-Publication Data is available upon request.

ISBN 978-0-7653-8845-2 (hardcover)
ISBN 978-0-7653-8846-9 (e-book)

Our books may be purchased in bulk for promotional, educational, or business use. Please contact your local bookseller or the Macmillan Corporate and Premium Sales Department at 1-800-221-7945, extension 5442, or by e-mail at MacmillanSpecialMarkets@macmillan.com.

First Edition: February 2017

Printed in the United States of America

0 9 8 7 6 5 4 3 2 1

To a real-life hero with the same last name as the one I invented: Dale L. Walker (1935–2015), whose sly wit, fierce intelligence, and warm friendship I will miss all the days of my life. We'll meet again around the campfire one day.

When lions hunt together it is usually the lioness
which leads them.

—Kalman Kittenberger, *Big Game Hunting and
Collecting in East Africa, 1903–1926*

THE LIONESS
IS THE HUNTER

ONE

The receptionist parted her cranberry-colored hair in the middle and showed a gap between her front teeth when she smiled. I'm a sucker for little imperfections like that. I wanted to feed nickels into that slot all day, just to watch her lights blink on. Instead I gave her a card.

"Mr. Fannon asked me to meet him here. He's catching a plane or something after the interview." Important people are always catching planes. Why they have to chase them at all is a mystery I'll have to solve on my own time.

She read the card, but all she got from it was my name. I have another set with my contact numbers and the service I provide for when I'm drumming up business. She didn't strike me as a customer.

She glanced at the big electric clock on the wall. "He should be free in a few minutes. Please take a seat."

I found one upholstered in orange vinyl opposite a city councilman I'd helped out of a jam once involving an aide who got caught carrying an unregistered revolver through the Detroit-Windsor Tunnel. The councilman was wearing an empty holster on his belt when they were pulled over, but I knew someone in Customs and that part didn't get as far as the MacNamara Federal Building.

The councilman, a skinny jasper wearing a heavy gold U-of-D class ring and hair implants, was too busy reading papers from a briefcase to look up and recognize me. He probably wouldn't have anyway, without someone to whisper my name in his ear.

A thick glass partition separated us from a round table where two men wearing headsets were leaning into lozenge-shaped microphones. That room was soundproof, but a square speaker mounted on a wall piped their voices into the waiting room.

"Carl Fannon, scuttlebutt says you're planning to add our home to your holdings. Would you care to confirm that for our listeners?"

"Paul, all I can tell you right now is we're in negotiations."

"You heard it here first, ladies and gentlemen. How about a raise, boss?"

The man seated across from the radio host chuckled. He had a smooth baritone designed for gentle humor in public, and blistering dressings-down in the privacy of some corner office. He wore a mulberry-colored suit with a thin silver stripe that matched his hair where he cropped it close to the temples. His eyes were gray ball-bearings in a narrow face as tan as toast.

The suit hung well no matter how he moved. Just sitting there he represented six months' income for me.

The host's tone darkened a shade. "Correct me if I've lost track, but I think this will bring Velocity Financing's properties in Detroit to seventy. How do you and your partner,

Emil Haas, respond to accusations you're fronting for foreign interests, selling out our city overseas?"

"Now you sound like Cecil Fish." Fannon's voice retained its silken tone, but now a steel thread ran through it. Even the councilman looked up from his papers.

"Heaven forbid. Here we endeavor to strike a positive note in all things."

"You succeed, regardless of the subject matter."

The host beamed as if he'd been complimented. "We have to check in on the news. Thank you, Carl Fannon, and Velocity Financing for your efforts to bring back Detroit."

"Well, that's what we're here for, isn't it."

A molasses-voiced newsman ticked off the day's tragedies, punctuated by traffic updates and ten solid minutes of varicose veins and auto dealerships. In a bulletin, the host reported a murder, smacking his lips over a bowl of free ice cream from a sponsor.

Bottled water filled a basket on a coffee table in front of me. It tasted like drool. The same brand filled a cooler in the corner and ten percent of the advertising slots. All the place lacked was a glad-hander in a straw hat out front, slapping backs and roping in customers.

I rose simultaneously with the city councilman when Carl Fannon emerged from the fishbowl. The entrepreneur stopped briefly for a word with the receptionist, who passed him my card. The next interviewee took a moment to shake Fannon's hand with both of his.

"Hack." Fannon pocketed my card while the councilman went into the inner sanctum. "You're Walker?"

"That's the rumor. You give good PR. How's chances you've really got this place in inventory?"

"None whatsoever. It's too healthy. We specialize in hopeless properties; if nothing comes of them, we can always write them off, and say the deal fell through. Meanwhile we've sucked all we can out of the headlines. Do you mind walking and talking? I'm on my way to Metro."

Out in the hall we passed a row of framed blow-up photographs of the station's stars. None of them looked like they sounded.

The elevator was a Deco affair like the rest of the building, bronze-plated with a faux marble floor no car would have supported if it were genuine, and the building itself reproduced in mosaic tile on the back wall. The hydraulic mechanism hummed like a factory hybrid under a steady stream of White Stripes covers. "I've got a town car," Fannon said. "Okay if we continue this on the way to the airport? I'll have the driver take you anywhere you want afterward."

"Vegas would be good. I've got the morning free, Mr. Fannon."

He dealt himself a miniature cigar from a foil-covered box and played with it. "I got your name from Lieutenant Stonesmith in Missing Persons. She was honest enough not to offer any guarantees the regular force could keep this under wraps. The whole town's drunk on transparency since the Kilpatrick Administration."

"Just the print media," I said. "The guy who just interviewed you handled that crook with oven mitts."

"And all that time he couldn't turn a corner without hearing the rumors. That's why stations like this are where we take our trade. I can keep lobbing those Nerf ball questions over the net in my sleep." He smoothed the cigar between his fingers. "What do you expect? It's not their town, for all the flag-waving. They finish up their four-hour shift and go home to their gated communities in the suburbs. They can't even vote here."

"Don't be too hard on them. They've got people to answer to."

"You don't. I got that from the lieutenant; not that it sounded like any kind of compliment."

"I'm not popular down there. I'm not popular at all, Mr. Fannon."

"Thank God for that. That dodo who shook my hand upstairs won re-election by better than sixty percent, and I wouldn't trust him to check my overcoat."

The doors slid open and we passed down a cool marble corridor—the real thing—that smelled of buffed wax and disinfectant like vanilla extract, then out into a parking lot roasting under a brutal Michigan summer sun. The parked cars shimmered in streamers of heat reflecting off the asphalt. A chauffeur leaning his hips against a polished black fender came alive, ditched his stub, and swung open a rear door for his passengers. I caught a whiff of cannabis off his blazer. We climbed into a backseat upholstered in tan glove leather. "Delta terminal," directed Fannon.

Tinted Plexiglas separated us from the driver. Fannon rapped on it lightly, and when the man behind the wheel didn't act as if he'd heard, sat back and set fire to his cigar with a gold butane lighter, which he offered me. I shook my head, leaving my pack of Winstons in my pocket; the exhaust from his smoke saved me the price of a butt. We passed my Cutlass baking in its slot. At that hour of the morning the dusty interior wouldn't be any harder to take than a tour of Cairo; but it was a ninety-minute round trip from

Detroit Metropolitan Airport to a parking lot on Grand. For the hundredth time I considered investing in one of those foil windshield screens that are all the rage in Arizona.

On Michigan, Fannon pointed his cigar through the window on his side at a pile stretching eighteen stories high, all fluted granite with a spire on top that had been designed to moor dirigibles during the lighter-than-air craze of the 1930s. The spire had never been used, thanks to the *Hindenburg*. Most of the mullioned windows were boarded over, with gang signs spray-painted as high as the eleventh floor. An unsightly black smear showed where a scrap rat had electrocuted himself trying to strip copper wire from a light pole on the corner three months ago. A motorist on his way to work had reported the charred corpse dangling twenty feet above the pavement.

"The Sentinel Building," Fannon said. "Know much about it?"

"Built during the construction boom of the twenties, on twenty millions on margin on the New York Stock Exchange, with pink Carrara in the restrooms, a waterfall in the lobby, and brass cherubim peeing off the roof. All those stories of stockbrokers throwing themselves from the top floor on Black Friday are myth; but urban legends tell more truth than the facts."

"It's had its moments. Studebaker kept some of its corporate offices there until it went belly-up, and there was a rumor the first female president of GM's Oldsmobile division would relocate there with her staff. Anyone could have predicted the model was doomed when the board of directors relented and put a woman in charge. You can always blame a skirt when the pot-bellied brass drops the ball."

I powered down the window on my side; the smoke from his cigar was making me woozy. "Is this history lesson going to take long? There was so much less of it to learn when I was in college."

Fannon twirled his cigar between his fingers like a baton, then extinguished it in the chromium tray set into the armrest on his side. Immediately he broke out another, but he didn't fire it up.

"We're going to buy the building," he said, fingering his lighter without flicking it into flame. "Turn it into high-rise condominiums. Or we were, until Emil Haas dropped off the face of the earth."

"People do, Mr. Fannon. That's how I pay the rent."

TWO

There are competing bidders," he said, "including an emir, a pimply dot-com fatcat, and that bleeding-heart back East who says his kind doesn't pay enough taxes and runs a stable of tax lawyers to make sure he doesn't. But the papers are all drawn up and okayed by both sides; even the unions are on board. All it needs is Emil's signature, and he's chosen now of all times to go dark."

"He's done it before?"

"Six years ago. But he was going through a rotten divorce, and who can blame a man for keeping a roomful of family-service attorneys cooling their heels while he sits drinking in some dive?"

"Is he an alcoholic?"

"I've never seen him take a drink. I'm just saying I'd understand if he got drunk under those circumstances. His daughter finally found him in an Internet café, reorganizing the company's computer files on his laptop."

"Check the place this time?"

"I tried his loft on the river first. The neighbors haven't

seen him. The café had closed, but I sent people to all the others in the area: No one there recognized him from his description. I'm worried. He always gets keyed up just before a closing, as many times as we've been through it, but he's never run out on one of those before."

I asked when he saw Haas last.

"Friday, four days ago. We'd just left a meeting with the owners of the Sentinel and their lawyers. They were going to have the papers drawn up over the weekend and we'd be back in their offices yesterday for the signing. Emil shook my hand outside the office. He said he was taking his daughter out to lunch. They had reservations at the Blue Heron, but she says she waited in the restaurant for him an hour and a half and he never showed. She was pretty unpleasant about it; I take it he'd stood her up before."

"I had to cancel the signing," he went on, "and the owners weren't pleasant about that. The lawyers think we're stalling to whittle down the price we agreed on."

"What's the daughter's name?" I got out my pad.

"Gwendolyn Haas; at least I think she went back to her maiden name after her own divorce. I doubt she can tell you anything she didn't tell me, but Brita will tell you where she can be reached. Carl and I have adjoining offices in the Parker Block. Brita keeps us from tripping over our own shadows." He switched hands on his cigar and broke a slate-colored card out of a leather-bound case with his initials embossed on it.

I fondled the heavy pebbled stock. The *V* in Velocity Financing, sans-serif in outline, leaned radically to the right with wind-lines running through it. I stuck the card in the pad.

"I'll need more."

"Brita can give you everything you require. I'll be in Beijing the rest of the week." He looked sideways at me. "That pest Fish thinks anyone who ever got within spitting distance of the Great Wall is selling us out to the reds. China's our country's creditor, for God's sake. Give it a rest."

"I know Fish. You could buy him off for less than the ground floor of that wreck on Michigan."

"Why should I?"

"No reason, Mr. Fannon. What I don't know about your business would fill every vacant lot in this city."

We followed the oval track around the airport to the Delta terminal, where Wayne County Sheriff's deputies were directing traffic six deep. The driver slid into a loading zone on the rear bumper of a minivan wheeling out, pulled a two-suiter on rollers and a leather duffel from the trunk, and opened the door on Fannon's side. He let the driver wait while he got out a long flat wallet that matched his card case and handed me a cashier's check with the amount of my retainer spelled out in perforated characters.

"I'm beginning to think I made the right choice." He put one foot on the pavement. "I like a man who says, 'I don't know.' Do you have any idea how many people I meet who'd never admit that?"

"I don't know."

He frowned, got out, and shut the door in my face. I got the impression I'd said the wrong thing; but then I wouldn't know.

Back on I-94 the driver ran down the partition and asked if I wanted to stop anyplace on the way back to town. I caught a strong whiff of reefer from the front seat. I inhaled deeply, grinned, and said, "No, thanks. Just keep the window open."

The work sounds interesting, but the pattern's as steady as a square dance: I deposit the check, keeping a couple of hundred out for bail and gasoline, and go back to the office to make arrangements to see the people I need to see in order to earn it. The people in Carl Fannon's set are never impressed by calls made over cell phones that break up when you drive under a low-flying pigeon, so I passed through the stale air lock that is my reception room, unlocked the door to the Holy See, and used the landline on the desk. Sitting back waiting for someone to answer I contemplated the dark smear of extinct arthropods in the bowl of the ceiling fixture. The cleaning service came with the rent or I'd raise a stink about the way the Dustbusters never got higher than the chair rail.

A cozy little box, inside the larger box of a building that should have been torn down under Woodrow Wilson, in the larger box yet of a city that should have been condemned after the '67 riots and replaced with a theme park devoted to the Underground Railroad. It came with my entire working life contained in ten green steel drawers, a fiberboard-framed print made from a historically inaccurate painting of a military disaster that could have been avoided with a little more firepower and a lot less ego, a Native American rug woven in the Republic of Indonesia, and a leatherette-upholstered chair mounted on a screw behind a desk that still contained the holes from where a pencil sharpener had stood on it in what was probably the same grammar-school class where I'd flunked Algebra; and what of that? So had Einstein. A rotary fan danced on the sill of the open window and made visible wrinkles in the air; it was that thick in Michigan in housefly season.

But even a steady pattern can throw you a curve now and then. A crisp feminine voice with a West End accent came on the line, asked if I could hold, and before I could answer handed me over to a Baroque concert. I was adding up the counterpoints in a fugue when someone knocked.

I called out an invitation. He opened the door just wide enough to sidle in around it, as if he were afraid it might bump into someone standing on the other side. That made him the brains of the outfit, probably; the really smart ones spend their lives in a constant state of apology.

He was big, that much was obvious; not hard, but not suety either, just a larger than usual helping of humanity. The effect of bigness was lost in his general attitude. Although he was dressed as expensively as Carl Fannon, the best tailoring can't really hang from a frame like his without looking like some kind of apron. He had short curly whitish hair that clung to his head like a knitted cap, and was as pale as my client was tan. His skin had a sickly translucence, like the skin that forms on scalded milk. He would apply sunscreen with a trowel. I'd never seen a photograph of him, but the quality of his suit and his famous diffidence and most of all the timing told me who he was. I'm no Amazing Kreskin, but I'm good at my job.

He was practically transparent. It explained why he needed a rooster like Fannon to strut his bright feathers and crow for the benefit of the admiring public. Vision and a good head for figures weren't enough anymore; not in a society where the media sharks cut themselves in on everything as equal partners.

I cradled the receiver. "Thanks for dropping in, Mr. Haas. You just saved your firm a boatload in expenses."

THREE

He slid the client's chair away from the desk, using both hands, and lowered himself onto it with a big sigh, as if he'd taken in too much breath for the job and had to blow some of it off. The chair wasn't that heavy and he wasn't that fat, but the effort on top of climbing two flights of stairs had sapped him plenty. He had bulk and not enough strength to lug it far. He was like a plant someone had over-fertilized so that it grew too big too fast and wouldn't last the season.

His voice was high and shallow. I had to lean forward to hear him. "Stop looking for me," he said. "Am I lost?"

"Disoriented, maybe. I get a lot of that in here."

"Well, I'm not that, either. I may not look like it, but I know where I am all the time and why."

"I believe you. Now tell me and we'll both know."

"Our office manager is my main pipeline. I recruited her from the secretarial pool over Carl's objections. He wanted a flashy blonde to rope in business. That's back when Hollywood incentives were in place here; he thought we could unload a couple of hundred thousand square feet of dud industrial property we had in inventory to a pack of C.B. DeMilles to build studios. He's changed his mind since Lansing threw out the incentives; but Brita's loyalty's still to me."

"Brita isn't a name I associate with an office drudge. Parents are prescient about such things. They rarely look at an Ethel in the cradle and christen her Brita."

"Oh, she's damn attractive, from the front row. Carl wanted something that would play to the balcony, all chrome and lacquer. But ours isn't the kind of business you conduct at a distance. It's long hours of discussing tedious details over buckets of coffee and long columns of figures. People like Brita take the edge off; she makes a tailored business suit look like a slinky ball gown." His face shut down then; not that it had opened up more than a morning glory an hour before dawn. "Plus she can tell at a glance whether the customer's the real deal or a looky-loo."

"Good-looking women can," I said. "That's how they keep their good looks."

The air outside was just heavy enough with humidity to carry sounds a long way, like across a calm lake; the fan brought them in along with the air from the street, syrupy sweet with fresh tar patch in the potholes. Tires splatted against asphalt, stereo speakers grunted pure bass, the wheels of a child's stroller clicked over joints in the sidewalk, the traffic light at the intersection passed through its cycle with discernible clicks. A car alarm went off. No city medley is complete without that.

"Brita's the one who made our appointment," I said. "I'm guessing." She hadn't identified herself by name, but I remembered a cool mid-Atlantic voice that made an invitation sound like a done deal.

"I could recite the conversation word-for-word," Haas said. "Carl never does anything I don't know about, thanks to her. You might say she's the cement that holds the partnership together."

"Cement sticks both ways, you know."

He lifted pale brows. Only the faint shadows cast by the bristles separated them from the skin of his forehead.

"You're suggesting she'd two-time me. She might, if I ever did anything my partner thought would hurt the business. As it happens, I *am* the business. I control the money, I make the deals, my signature closes the decisions. Carl books hotels, arranges companionship, and spreads oil on the waters where the media dips its bill."

"Like with that pushover at the radio station?"

"He didn't have to. Why does the city bother having a chamber of commerce when that crew does the job for free?"

"There's always a Carl, isn't there?"

"It's a special skill. Just because I don't possess it myself doesn't mean I think his contribution is less important than mine." He sat back as far as he allowed himself, gripping the arms of the wooden chair with his thick sausage fingers; they would leave wet marks. "He's distinguished, looks well in his clothes, and has a pleasant speaking voice. I consider that natural compensation for his deficiency in other areas."

That was generous. Most Brainiacs saw it the other way around. "Why does he think you're vanished?"

He scowled. "Terrible misuse of a verb. I took a room under an alias in the kind of motel where no one would ever look for me who knew my phobias. Not a fleabag; that desperate I'm not, but let's say the chain it belongs to doesn't advertise on *Sixty Minutes*. I thought it better to lie low and say nothing than postpone our meeting with the Sentinel people. I'd rather the mystery be about what hole I fell into than why I had misgivings."

"What kind of misgivings?"

He shifted in his chair, winding up in the same position he'd started in. He seemed to live in a constant state of armed truce with his clothes and his environment, and possibly with the world in general. He was either a genius or a crackpot. I'd entertained both in that room, sometimes occupying the same chair at the same time. "Before I go into that, I need some assurance you won't go running to your client with it."

"He didn't buy that, only some line on where you went off to. We didn't discuss when I'd report."

His chair creaked a little more, but this time he was just making room to fetch a billfold from his hip pocket. It was fat, brown, and tattered, with corners of currency and printed receipts and little colored tabs sticking out at all angles; I'd as soon have carried around a dead porcupine. He extracted a sheaf of bills and stood them on the desk in the shape of a tent. "That's fifteen hundred." He sat back holding the billfold on his lap in both hands like a woman's handbag. "That's your initial rate, isn't it?"

"It's my special introductory offer." I didn't move to scrape it up. "What am I selling?"

"Just twelve hours' silence regarding this visit; and the promise to meet me tonight someplace where I know we won't be overheard."

"Strictly speaking, it's legal until Fannon's retainer expires, in three days minus a couple of hours and change."

"We have an arrangement, then?"

I drew a new yellow pencil from the mug on the desk, navy blue with the Detroit Police Officers Association seal in gold; the department keeps a little gift shop on the floor of 1300 Beaubien, police headquarters, and gives them out when it's feeling generous. I'd swiped mine from an interview room. The pencil was for tapping, not writing. I thumped the eraser on the blotter three times, then tilted forward, picked up the tent, and separated a twenty from it.

"This will cover my time, if we're meeting anywhere in this area code. Keep the rest for seed and we'll see if it sprouts tonight. Your room?"

"God, no. I've been sleeping on the coverlet. I'm afraid to touch even the light switches without wrapping my hands in Kleenex; which I brought in myself in the handy little packet Walmart sells in the travel section at a markup of three-hundred-fifty percent. You know where the Sentinel Building is, of course. Knowing Carl, he'd have been sure to take you past it on his way to the airport."

"I know it anyway. My old man used to buy me candy cigarettes in the cigar shop when he went in to play the numbers. Can we get in?" I seemed to remember yellow caution tape across the entrance.

"Carl and I hired a crew to check the place out for structural failure. You don't need to worry about rats; they're too smart to hang around a place with no food. There's a trouble-light setup in the basement, and I have a key to the fire door in the alley. I made a copy." He reached inside the

billfold again and slid something across the desk: flat copper with a round blank tab. "Nine o'clock?"

"You haven't told me what the job is."

He'd hoisted himself out of the chair. Now he tugged
some of the wrinkles out of his clothes and touched a thick
moist lower lip with the corner of the billfold, thinking
through his answer. He was a man who'd give you the time
of day, after confirming it with his watch, his cell, Green-
wich, and the U.S. Naval Observatory.

"Nothing extravagant: just a background check. I could
run it myself, but you can't travel three inches across a computer monitor without leaving a trail of blinking lights. The
check I tried to do on you came up empty from here to Sili-
cone Valley and back. How does a man in your profession
manage to stay off the grid in this century?"

"I crashed my first Etch A Sketch at ten. After that technology and I shook hands and said good-bye."

He smiled then. Before that it had seemed to be one
symbol not included in his personal emoticon.

"Which makes you the man for me. You leave no foot-
prints and fly six feet under the radar. When your time
comes, there'll be no evidence you even existed. Please for-
give me if I upset you by saying that."

"I'm not so delicate as that, Mr. Haas."

He frowned again. The thin latex of his skin wouldn't
stand up to much of that strain.

"If I seem circumspect, it's the life I've led. I have the ad-
vantage of being an unattractive man. When a beautiful
woman comes to someone like me with a proposition, I'm
not deluded into thinking my good looks and charm have

anything to do with it. There's always something else. The same reasoning applies to business. A deal that looks too good to be true—is. This Sentinel acquisition is just the latest in a long line of such things. If Carl weren't so persuasive I'd have gone with my instincts three deals ago, and sixteen million dollars to the good."

I smiled as if I knew what he was talking about: Just two movers and shakers discussing business that affected the lives of hundreds. In the back of my mind I remembered my oil needed changing.

I stood and shook his hand, which was firmer than I expected and just firm enough to make me worry about what it had cost him, and watched him shamble on out, a man built like a bear, but who moved like a squirrel, hoping to cross the road before a car ran him over. Watching the door drift shut behind him I slid the twenty between two fingers to smooth out the crease and put it in my inside pocket next to the two hundred I'd kept out from Carl Fannon's grand-and-a-half. I had a sudden urge to catch the red-eye to Atlantic City; but I had an appointment to keep in eleven hours.

FOUR

What do you do with eleven hours to kill and no more credit at the corner liquor store?

I hadn't had work in a month. The Internet had swooped in and snatched up all the jobs I used to do, free of charge. You could track down an old high school sweetheart, a deadbeat dad, your great-great-great-grandfather's crib in the Old Country, complete with a virtual walking tour of his thatched hut. No phone time, no embarrassing conversation with a stranger, and best of all no bill. A couple more months like the last and I'd be calling people up at suppertime pitching time shares in New Mexico.

I could get a computer and learn to use it, but what was the point, if everyone else had one? My special skills were all I had to offer, and anyone with a tablet thought he had them already.

Oh, there was work to be had, as long as there were people left who cared about privacy. The concept itself was alien to a generation that posted its bong parties on Facebook and trashed the boss for everyone to read on the social network. Spouses went missing, sons and daughters too, and the clients in those cases weren't interested in sharing the details with the neighborhood gossip. There was enough of that sort of work to keep me in cigarettes and sandwiches for the rest of my span, if I kept to a carton a week and didn't look too closely at what went into the bologna.

I couldn't remember when was the last time an Arabian princess had smuggled herself into my office rolled up in an Oriental rug or an accountant for the mob had sent me a stack of ledgers by parcel post To Be Called For or I'd found a tarantula swimming laps in my bowl of Frosted Flakes. My daily dose of danger had become a seasonal thing.

On the other hand, I couldn't remember when was the last time I'd landed two clients in one day, and it was only midmorning. That they both had to do with the same case belonged in that column with the widow in Sioux Falls who'd hit the Powerball for millions twice. Or maybe it cut the odds to fifty-fifty; if I were good at math I'd know the probabilities against making a living in my profession.

She had nothing on me, though, that old lady in South Dakota. My telephone rang before Emil Haas reached the street.

"A. Walker Investigations."

"Amos Walker, please." A woman's voice, mezzo range.

"Speaking."

"Oh."

That was the usual reaction. I never knew what that meant, whether the caller was expecting a cool female receptionist or a menu: Press One for Cheating Spouse, Two for Crooked Partner, Three for Foreign Assassinations,

Four for Credit Checks. Some kind of go-between. I should get one, but I don't think the building could handle another landline.

Whatever it was, she recovered herself in a heartbeat. "My name is Gwendolyn Haas. My father is Emil Haas. Perhaps you've heard of him?"

I'd lit a cigarette before lifting the receiver. It burned to my fingers while I picked up the new yellow pencil. "Spell it, please."

She was a redhead; the genuine article, unlike the cranberry-dyed specimen at the radio station. The complexion's always the giveaway, blue-white, like skim milk, something inherited from her father; if Emil Haas was her father. At first glance I was inclined to put that one on the back burner. She treated my door like a door, not like a possibly threatening stranger she had to maneuver her way around, and the olive-green suit she wore made an expert combination with her deep auburn bob and brilliant green eyes. She was just the least bit too thick in the waist and broad in the hips for my taste, but I wasn't trolling for feminine companionship that season.

She slid out the customer's chair with nothing like the effort Emil Haas had put into it, sat down, crossed her legs, and rested her hands on a burgundy leather handbag with a gold clasp and no designer label in sight. It was just big enough to hold the usual items and a Glock Nine, but not a sleeping bag and a bazooka.

"Gwendolyn Haas," I greeted; "on approval."

"What's that mean?" It was the same voice I'd heard on the phone. The choir director would place her in the back row opposite the altos.

"I'd like to see some ID. I've been fooled before."

"Oh, for—" But she jerked open the handbag and passed over a plastic folder containing a driver's license and two credit cards. She'd smiled for the photographer at the Secretary of State's office, but the specimen in front of me passed just the same. I thanked her and handed back the folder.

"What can I do for you, Miss Haas? Or is it Ms.? I'm rusty on Emily Post and divorce."

"Who's Emily Post?"

"A woman I investigated for murdering all her husbands. When she served fish she put the arsenic in white wine."

"Miss is fine."

"That's fine. I'm fine, too. Everything's fine."

"Are you all right?"

"I will be, I hope. I've had a shock. Apparently it's ongoing."

She didn't like that. That was also fine. I didn't like her either, on no evidence at all. Life can be like that. I stopped questioning it a long time ago.

"My father stood me up for lunch last week. I'm used to that, but I don't have to enjoy it. I stewed about it all weekend, then when I couldn't reach him at his home I tried his office. His partner, Carl Fannon, said he'd get back to me, and when he didn't, I called back. The office manager said he was away on business. She didn't want to tell me anything else, but I kept at her until she got exasperated and said I should talk to you. I thanked her and said good-bye."

"As long as everything's civil."

"It's an ordeal. Those cool perfect beauties rub me the wrong way. Everything in this world just falls into their laps."

"Not Brita's fault. It's hereditary, like money."

She really didn't like that, and almost said so. She changed her mind. "How'd you know her name's Brita?"

"I'm a detective."

"If you've spoken with her, you must be working for Velocity. You know, it's no wonder you don't have a nicer office in a better neighborhood. You can't get much business treating customers the way you do."

"You're not a customer yet. I'm sorry, Miss Haas, but I can't discuss current work with just anybody. If you're worried about your father, I'll be glad to ask around."

"Wouldn't that be taking money from two different clients doing the same work? Is that ethical?"

I grinned and lit a cigarette. She didn't like that either, but she didn't say anything about the state law regarding places of business. I disliked her a little less for that. "You ought to apply for a license," I said. "If making a bald end run like that ever works."

"What do you mean?"

"If I defended opening a missing-persons investigation on someone I was already looking for, you'd conclude I've been hired to look for your father. If I fell for that one, I wouldn't be able to pay the freight on even this hole. The police can do what I do better and without charge, but their records are public property. That's what put the private in 'private detective.'"

Even I thought that was harsh. I put out the butt and

fanned the smoke away from the vicinity. "Let's start over, shall we?"

"Let's."

"When was the last time you saw your father?"

When she screwed up her face to think, freckles dived into the creases. "A month, I should say. He's been busy on some deal. That's nothing new, of course; there's always something big doing at Velocity, but this one must be more important than most, because I usually hear from him more regularly, usually briefly and by phone. We go out to lunch—when he remembers—and he tries to be the concerned parent when life hasn't been good to me. He was the rock I leaned on during my divorce, giving me moral support and offering to help me out financially, without bad-mouthing the other party or worse, reminding me I should have listened to his advice the first time. Of course, he had his own failures in that department, but I try to cut him some slack on the other. Like a lot of people with so much going on upstairs, he doesn't find much room in it for social bonding."

All I'd asked was when she'd seen him last.

"I'm worried," she said. "He's not quite the absentminded genius who can suss out the mistakes in Newton's theory of the universe and gets lost changing buses, but the cutthroats he traffics with in the world of mergers and acquisitions have nothing on the sort of people who cut your throat for real. For all I know he pulled into an alley to argue a clause in some contract and got himself carjacked while he was too busy texting to pay attention to what was going on around him."

"You tried to reach him?"

"Of course. He doesn't answer any of his phones or messages, and when I went to see him at his condo on the river I wore out my thumb on the doorbell. His neighbors weren't any help; he's only been living there a few weeks, and it's the kind of building where everyone's forted up in his own affairs."

She'd taken a handkerchief from her bag; not to wipe away tears she hadn't shed, but just to have something to twist between her hands. Ten thousand dollars in orthodontia gnawed at her lower lip. Of a sudden she seemed to realize what she was doing, stopped both operations, and looked directly at me. "I saw your display in the Yellow Pages; I had to turn my place upside down to see if I still had one. You don't advertise online. You specialize in tracing people, so I thought—"

"I also check credit histories and guard the gift table at weddings in Grosse Pointe. This isn't New York or L.A.; there isn't so much work lying around I can afford to turn up my nose at anything, except divorce cases." I used a little finger to rearrange the butts in the tray so they didn't reignite one another, and in the doing made a decision.

"It so happens I am working for your father's partner. If in the course of talking to the people I have to talk to and going to the places I have to go I learn anything about Emil Haas, I'll pass it along—after I've filed my report. Will that do?"

"It's better than nothing. Oh!" She opened the bag again and rummaged around inside.

"No charge," I said. "You'd be surprised what a fellow can make sitting on a toaster oven in Barbie's Dreamhouse on Lake Shore Drive. The people that boost those places aren't the same lunks that drive pickups into gas stations and make off with the ATM, so I hike my rates when I cross Eight Mile Road."

"Who," she said.

"Say again?"

"It's 'people who,' not 'people that.' I make my living teaching grammar to professional communicators. I work, despite that crack you made about inherited wealth."

She was her father's daughter, all right; it was my second English lesson that day. "If you start splicing my infinitives, I may change my mind about a fee."

She produced a checkbook.

"Joke," I said. "You're right about my sense of humor. It's a plus on the street and a minus in the parlor."

She dropped it back into the bag and snapped shut the clasp. "Is it possible I've misjudged you?"

"I hope so, Miss Haas. The job's easier when people do. That's another reason I don't keep a ficus in the office or the office in Bloomfield Hills."

She gave me a number in the Oakland County exchange and an address in a suburb I had to wash and wax my car in to keep the local cops off my rear bumper. When she went out, leaving me with an aroma of night-blooming berries I hadn't noticed all the time she was there, I sat back and looked at my watch. The hands were straight up. The day was only half over and I had more work than I'd seen since the last snow.

FIVE

They'd built a translucent plastic tunnel over the sidewalk in front of the Sentinel Building, to protect strollers from falling gargoyles and such; which had as usual the effect of steering pedestrians to the other side of the street. A sudden shady stretch in broad daylight is nothing to sneer at in our city. Thousands of mosquitoes can breed in a teaspoon of water, and a hundred muggers and rapists in a city block of shadow.

It was an impressive pile by most standards, designed they said by a student of Albert Kahn, the visionary whose Deco-neo-classical-Gothic wet dreams had rebuilt all downtown during the delirious twenties. But the master had disinherited it for its leaky roof and a structural failure that shattered the upper windows in a stiff breeze; Kahn was one of the last architects with engineering experience. Decades of costly reconstruction had resolved most of those issues, and the fluted tea-colored limestone and rows of windows fashioned after the mitre of the Archbishop of Canterbury made a bold statement against, say, the cylindrical glass towers of the Renaissance Center, built in the Disco era along the lines of a six-pack of Zima.

But ten years of racial unrest followed by four solid decades of corrupt government and incompetent reform had emptied all the rooms and placed the building on the national register of Who Cares. A parade of potential buyers had come with brass bands and excited local talk-show hosts, and gone on the back end of the weather report.

The prevailing mood was to level it and add yet another empty lot to a city that already looked as if a tornado had hopscotched across it, snapping its tail at this house, that corner market, leaving a square of crabgrass next door to practically everyone. The natives shot BBs at pheasants over their back fences, ten blocks from General Motors.

Yellowing placards in all the windows on the ground floor declared the place off-limits; but not to someone with a key to the fire door in the alley. This was a slab of red-painted steel flanked on one side by a pile of dirty laundry with a man wearing it, spooning yogurt out of a plastic cup, and on the other by the Dumpster where in all probability he'd found it. I rolled a dollar bill around a finger and poked it into a pocket of the fisherman's vest he wore over a tattoo of the *Edmund Fitzgerald*.

"Thank you, brother. Tha's half a package of wieners at Kroger. Frank's the name. Ain't that a stitch?"

"Okay, Frank. Just don't shoot up in the parking lot."

I inserted the key Emil Haas had given me, but the lock was a stranger to it. I pulled it out and examined it. It was a rough copy of the original, which had worn along with the tumblers. Whoever had duped it had neglected to file the edges. The raw shavings glittered in the sun. I scraped off what I could with my thumb and tried again, hauling back on the brass handle at the same time. The door sprang open so suddenly I had to turn my shoulder to keep it from smacking me in the face.

Inside was darkness, sliced into slivers by gray light leaking in around the plywood in the windows, and a musk of old wood and rodent droppings. I took out my pencil flash and switched it on. The beam shot out through a smoke of dust, stirred up by the current of air I'd let in through the door. I eased it back into its frame, groped behind my back for the latch, and slid home the dead bolt. I was moving like a guilty man, but these things still seemed to make more noise than necessary.

More plywood had been laid atop the floor and fixed with miles of wide brown tape to protect the Pewabic tiles from hobnail boots. The wood creaked under my feet as I followed a long wide hallway and came out into the hub of the ground floor lobby.

There was more light here, but only because there were more windows whose boards didn't fit snug to the frames. They'd be leaded glass, diamond-shaped or hexagonal beveled panes no larger than reading lenses forming a honeycomb pattern. From the center of the ten-foot coffered copper ceiling hung an electric chandelier the size of a pool table, wrapped in tea-colored muslin fuzzy with dust. Elevators with copper doors, each crisscrossed with yellow CAUTION tape, occupied the wall beside a broad staircase rising between bronze gryphons and brass banisters to the mezzanine, where in times past a clerk with a carnation in his buttonhole had spread open the big ledger-like book and handed the guest a horsehair pen to register and a pair of black porters in plum-colored uniforms trimmed with gold braid waited to carry bags upstairs, the men selected to match each other, like the elevator doors. A lot of swirly green marble and burled walnut and exotic plants with fat leaves in copper pots sprinkled about, to cover the padding in the construction budget. All gone now.

The place hadn't entirely escaped the scavenging epidemic. The brass faceplates had been pried off the walls next to the elevators and the copper wiring attached to the controls carried away, leaving handy holes for an extinct generation of wasps to build their paper nests; in the end even the insects had given it up for better prospects.

It had been a bank with a vault built into the foundation when Coolidge was in knickerbockers, then a hotel up until the Crash, then home to a succession of corporate offices, and for a brief period when democracy was in jeopardy worldwide a combination recruitment center and strategic complex where old warriors wearing medals won on San Juan Hill shoved toy tanks and destroyers across big tables with long-handled sticks like croupiers used to rake in cash; which was just how the tables might have been employed when the Purple Gang leased two upper floors for a gambling hell during Prohibition. A building as experienced as a stately old whore and with enough character to populate a city, empty now.

If Carl Fannon's anxiety about his partner's whereabouts was genuine, there was a possibility Velocity Financing would be the first suitor not to bail out after it got its publicity fix. Most likely whatever they had in mind would involve a wrecking ball and a clean empty downtown site worth more for resale than a patch of real estate with an elderly structure cluttering it up. Buildings rise and fall, but there is only so much Planet Earth, and at the moment in Detroit it was going at closeout prices.

I added cigarette smoke to the drifting dust and crushed out the stub on plywood among burn craters left by speculators and squatters. Haas had said the inspection crew had had lights set up in the basement, which was where he'd be waiting. I found the door in a shallow alcove next to one of the elevators, with wood grain painted on the metal and a wire grid in a small square window with flaking letters reading AUTHORIZED PERSONNEL ONLY. It was unlocked, but it presented plenty of drag when I hauled on the handle. It would have been the door the bank employees had used to gain access to the vault.

I'd snapped off my flash; there was enough ambient light in the lobby to make it unnecessary, and although I had permission to be there I hadn't wanted to splash the beam around and attract the notice of a passing patrol unit and have to explain myself and empty the contents of my wallet. Now I put it back on, to make sure there were still steps for my feet.

There were, paved with ribbed brown rubber and dust bunnies that jumped up to greet me like neglected Chihuahuas. I ran into something invisible that wrapped itself around my face with almost intelligent intent. The cobweb might have been there for ten years or ten minutes; the spider that wove it wasn't paid by the hour. I swept it from my face and descended into a smell of damp unpainted concrete and more of that dry rat odor, as old as the last tenant's departure. Rats have a healthy sense of self-preservation; they never hang around where there's no food to be found.

Steep steps led to a surface the color of flypaper, but not sticky. The stuff had enough grit mixed into it to keep me from falling on my face, but just enough slickness to make it easier to sweep with a push broom; some janitor had rolled polyurethane over the slab with that purpose in mind. But that had been a long time ago. The top coat had begun to peel and pill, rolling under my heels and clinging to them in shreds so that I had to stop every couple of yards and scrape them off on the toe of the other shoe. A fishy smell of rancid shellac joined the general effluvium in the ten-foot-high space under the ground floor. Twelve would have been no less claustrophobic.

At regular intervals, plain steel posts scabbed with indoor rust supported the I-beams that kept the building from collapsing on my head. They looked to be sagging in the light of my flash, then they didn't; then they did. When I waved it back and forth they danced to a tune played by the string quartet on the *Titanic*. I had an idea how that panda cub had felt just before its mother rolled over it in the zoo. The Sentinel Building hadn't any more reason to want to crush me to death.

Well, it had stood this long, as had I for a good part of it. I trained the circle of light on the floor and followed it without looking up again: same wisdom as walking a tightrope over Niagara Falls, only in reverse.

Workers past had used the space to deposit demolished material. There were sheets of broken frosted ceiling panels, mounded heaps of dusty pink insulation I hoped wasn't asbestos, packing crates that from their stenciled labels had contained replacement fixtures made in China and imported on the cheap: Band-Aids slapped on mortal wounds to limp the place along until it was time for the negotiations to fall through.

The space seemed vast, more than twice the square footage of the ground floor. The flashlight's shaft didn't reach as far as the walls, creating an impression of limitless space. Finally it flattened out against a solid dimpled wall and I thought I'd gone as far as I could go. But I smelled a stench of burning dust and hot metal, as of a radiator that had overheated itself dry. I switched off the flash. When my eyes adjusted, I detected a dim source of light somewhere ahead and to my right, and saw a corridor leading that direction, where electric bulbs burned. I turned and walked toward the light.

SIX

The dry hot smell increased as I continued along the passage, as did the light of the bulbs that made it. I snapped off the flash and dropped it into my side pocket. Its shallow weight made me miss my revolver, but that was out of reach, in a drawer in my desk. I had a crazy urge to go back for the spare piece in the car, but I tamped it down. I was all grown up now, took spooky old basements in my stride.

The atmosphere underground wasn't as hot as above, but it was close and musty. I hadn't gone many steps when I began sweating. I seemed to be recycling my own spent breath. A once-busy building near the center of the business district in a once-bustling city is emptier than most when it's empty, and the space beneath it is emptier still. I was Howard Carter, wandering stone passages in search of the king's chamber, inhaling air that hadn't been breathed since a thousand years before Christ. It made me woozy.

"Get a grip, Walker."

I jumped at the sound of the voice echoing off the walls. My hand was halfway to the place where I carry a gun, when I carry a gun, when I realized the voice was mine.

When the hall opened into a room it was homely enough, more bare concrete with junk on the floor and across from me the dull shine of a six-by-three steel door. The handle opposite the hinges was a steel wheel with spokes on the outside, like a ship's helm. Back when amateur acrobats balanced on flagpoles, this would have been tempered titanium two feet thick standing between me and ten million dollars in bills, sacks of coins, and negotiable securities, and no one knew how much in privately rented safe-deposit boxes. The concrete itself would be steel-reinforced, with state-of-that-era's-art alarm sensors built in and connected to a direct telephone line to Detroit Police Headquarters. Now the wires would be corroded through, and if a message somehow managed to make it across town, a robo-operator would inform the robo-caller that the line was no longer in use (and hadn't been since the vault had held the box office receipts from *Son of the Sheik*).

A group of halogen lights wearing football face guards was clamped to a scaffold in the center of the floor. Quaintly, they were trained on the door of the vault. For the hell of it I stepped close and looked at the old-fashioned digital time display set in beside the steering-wheel handle, printed in black on individual curved yellow Bakelite tabs. Just as I leaned in to read the faded numerals through the grime coating them, one of them turned over with a click.

I jumped again.

The sound wasn't loud, but in the silence ten feet below

the sidewalk and unexpected as it was, someone might have blown up a paper sack and slapped it between his palms next to my ear.

Automatically I compared the time on the display to the watch strapped on my wrist. Two minutes' difference. I was prepared to believe I was the one behind.

Somebody—one of the inspectors, or maybe a partner—had killed a few minutes satisfying himself if the mechanism still worked by setting it. It was more than just doubtful it would have kept time since the first quarter of the last century all on its own. For one thing, I didn't think daylight savings time would have existed back when the League of Nations was sitting. The argument between the clock and my watch would have been an hour instead of a couple of minutes.

Or was that right? I had more important things to remember than whether it was "spring forward, fall back" or the other way around. Like making rent.

While I was putting my brain to such constructive use, another minute dropped into place with a click. Then something went thunk.

In its way it was quieter than the clicks, but that was because it had come from inside the ton of steel door.

There was a whir, then another thunk, and a sharp sliding snick of bolts gliding back into sockets.

This time I wasn't acting for the hell of it. I grasped two of the spokes belonging to the wheel and spun it clockwise. It rotated as smoothly as if it had been oiled just that day. The weight of the door started it my direction. I stepped back to keep it from hitting me in the face.

Wishing more than ever I'd gone back for that gun.

The great door drifted around silently on its hinges, slowed on a system of baffles, and sighed to a rest against the wall, quiet as the tide. If the vault was lighted, the bulb had burned out long ago, or the wires gone to corrosion. The halogens, on a separate circuit, were tilted slightly downward, their light falling three feet short of the back wall of the vault. I groped for the flash, changed hands on it twice to mop the greasy sweat off my palms, switched it on, and pointed it inside. A pile of sacks lay against the base of the back wall. They would be empty. The Depression had closed the bank. They'd have chased down every penny.

Just in case the door got any ideas about closing, I fetched a couple of packing crates and stacked them against it. The weight of it would fold them like gum wrappers, but they might slow it down long enough for me to climb out. I thought about that, then got some more crates and threw them on top of the others. Then I stepped over the rubber-gasketed threshold.

I wasn't John Dillinger. I'd never been inside a bank vault before and had no idea what to expect. It was larger than I might have guessed: It would have held all the furniture in my little reception room with space to spare. It was lined with metal boxes flush to the walls, with a steel butler's cart mounted on rubber casters for a clerk to roll out Henry Ford's pocket change. Any smell of money the place might have contained had evaporated around the time of Mick Jagger's First Communion, leaving behind an industrial order of smooth metal and 3-in-One oil; someone had lubricated the hinges and lock mechanism, and recently. I didn't know what to make of that. Someone had had more time on his hands than seemed fair.

I caught another scent then, of stale desperate sweat. It might have been my own, but belatedly I realized it had been there right along.

My toes came to the pile of sacks and touched something solid. My heart slid into my shoes. The air was close in an airtight chamber in summer, but the sweat on my face turned to ice water. I bent just far enough to grab hold of fabric and pull.

It didn't come free. It wasn't a sack at all, but a suit that would be mulberry-colored under ordinary light with a silver pinstripe. The face of the man wearing it was the same shade as the stripe, and it didn't belong to Emil Haas.

The last time I'd seen the suit, the man wearing it had been carrying two pieces of luggage into the Delta terminal at Detroit Metropolitan Airport, bound for Beijing. The face was turned toward the floor, but the short hair at the temples matched the stripe and the odds were against meeting two men in one day who could pull off the dark purple in between without looking like a circus barker.

I started to reach, stopped, then bit the bullet. I grasped him by the chin and turned his face my way. The muscles let me do that; they hadn't gone rigid yet. It was Carl Fannon all right. One eye was closed, the white of the other glistened through a half-moon of lifted lid. He wasn't seeing any more out of that one than its mate.

I knelt and pawed him with the beam of the flash from hairline to heels. No fresh holes in the exposed flesh, no bloodstains. I wasn't curious enough to turn him over all the way and explore further. I lifted one hand; the outside edge was bruised nearly the same shade of purple as his suit and swollen. The base of the nails were the identical color, and if anything darker.

Inspecting the other hand was pointless. He'd have hammered at the locked door with both fists, yelled himself hoarse, and when he'd abandoned that and used up all the oxygen in the vault, all ten nails would show the same sign of suffocation.

It could have been an accident. His firm was negotiating to buy the building, he'd been given permission to inspect it, had decided to check the place out himself, found the vault door open or unlocked, wandered inside without taking the precaution of blocking the door as I had, and it had drifted shut, locking automatically. I didn't know if the timer had to be reset by someone or if it went back to a default setting on its own; but there would be people who could answer that question.

It would take someone with other skills to find out how a man who should by then have been cruising over the Himalayas on the way to China wound up smothered to death in a disused bank vault ten feet under the streets of Detroit.

My jaw ached. I wondered why, then realized my teeth were still gritted. I opened my mouth and worked the jaw from side to side to loosen the muscles. Then I stood and poked the flash around, looking for a dying clue.

In detective stories there is often such a thing, when the victim has time to confirm the inevitability of death and also the urge to avenge himself. I'd never seen it myself, and I'd

been involved in that kind of murder case more times
than I thought wise to list on my résumé. For one thing, the
victim has to have had a good idea of his killer's identity.
Most do, but in those situations the party responsible is still
there when the police respond, holding the murder weapon
more often than not. The ones that keep the cops up nights
are usually committed by strangers, leaving the dying party
with a piece of chalk in his hand and nothing to write.

That's if he even thinks about writing anything.

I can't swear what I'd do in his shoes, but it seems to me
I'd be more interested in finding a way out. I'm willing to
bet that anyone who ever fell or was pushed off a tall building spent the time in freefall learning to fly.

But who was I to take issue with professional writers?
There is always a first time, even for a grizzled vet like me.
I prowled every inch of the space, looking for anything that
didn't belong there apart from a dead body.

I looked for something etched with a finger in the dust,
a message scratched with a thumbnail, a clever coded clue
using the objects at hand. If I was really on the ball, I'd have
chewed the murderer's name backwards into the rubber
casters of the rolling cart, so that if you dipped them in ink
and rolled them across a sheet of white butcher paper . . .

Carl Fannon hadn't done any of those things—or for that
matter taken out the gold pen clipped to the inside breast
pocket of his suitcoat and written it on the neat little pad
that matched it. The pages were blank.

Happening to spot the familiar bullet-shaped cap when
the coat fell open, I thought about something else. Today's
high-power executive never goes down the hall to the toilet
without carrying along any number of whiz-bang commu-

nication devices. I'd been thinking too old-fashioned; if he truly thought all was lost and wanted to hang it on some-one, his first inclination would be to note it on some gizmo like that.

Or call for help, if he could get a signal through all that steel and concrete.

I knelt again, patted his pockets, and found a flat pigskin wallet containing a book of American Express travelers' checks, the usual bling of metallic cards in stacked pockets, and a thick sheaf of crisp bills, which I didn't count because they preserve fingerprints like soft wax. I hadn't made up my mind yet whether I was going to report what I'd found, but cops are proprietary about such things as the victim's personal effects, and I wasn't exactly in their good books at the best of times. I wiped off the rest and put it back. No smartphone, tablet, PalmPilot, or Bluetooth within sight or touch.

I was sitting back on my heels, poking my tongue around my mouth like a man probing for a missing tooth, when something chimed, a merry little one-note that plastered me to the ceiling.

When I climbed back down, something was glowing in the dimness of the vault. I took Fannon's left wrist between thumb and forefinger, turned it, and looked at a brushed-silver watch on a crocodile strap, a Dick Tracy job that transmitted and received messages, turned off the iron at home, balanced your checking account, and when it had a chance even told you the time. The text on the glowing face was bright yellow against a sapphire-blue background. I could have read it in the center of a black hole.

SEVEN

knew how to play it then, at least off the first tee. After that it was anyone's game.

On the other hand, that first shot can determine the remaining holes. The trouble with mistakes is you have to make them first.

I took one last look at Carl Fannon. It seemed there ought to be something to say, but I hadn't known him long enough to make any sort of eulogy, or even to decide whether I liked him. Then I stepped outside, kicked the packing crates free of the door, and heaved. It didn't take much, just enough to get it started. After that it shut on its own. That was a point in favor of the accident theory, and of my foresight in blocking it to begin with. I had more faith in the latter.

In the light of the flash I studied the steering-wheel handle. It was made of nubbed steel. Offhand I didn't think an expert could lift a good print. In any case I wiped it with my handkerchief, destroying any hope of lifting one; more particularly of lifting mine. That was my first crime of the day, tampering with evidence, although it wasn't the first time I'd committed that one. Upstairs, I opened the fire door, peered up and down the alley like a character in a comic spy movie, saw no one, shut the door, and wiped off the handle. On the way back to my car I did the same thing with the key Haas had given me and leaned down to poke it through a grate into the storm drain in the gutter.

Back behind the wheel I looked around again. The street was deserted at that hour. I cranked on the motor and drove away. The perfect crime.

I thought.

Darkness chased me down the street. My watch told me all decent people should be in bed: Me, too. Everything always looks better in the morning, they say: But they haven't seen me before a shower, a shave, and a bowl of black coffee. I went home, scrounged supper from the refrigerator, chased it with twelve-week-old Scotch from the cabinet above the sink, and slept the sleep of the guilty. In the morning I felt hungry enough to fry a couple of eggs, until I turned one over sloppily and a half-moon of white glistened up at me like one of Carl Fannon's dead eyes. I dumped it in the trash and munched dry toast with my coffee.

I caught the news on the radio, but for once there was only one murder and it was the wrong one.

In the foyer of my building Rosecranz, the ancient super, was at the directory, prying snap-on letters loose from the brackets and flicking them contemptuously into the stiff leather pocket of his tool belt, like a gardener plucking horn-worms off a cabbage.

Watching him, I slid a cigarette between my lips, but

didn't light it. I hadn't enough saliva to hold it in place for such a dangerous operation. "Who bugged out this time?"

"Some millionaire," he said in his obsolete Russian accent. "Probably made his pile designing those web site things and moved into the RenCen, down the hall from the boss of General Motors. What do I know? He left me with a wastebasket full of shredded paper and a busted computer I got to call up somebody to come in and recycle it, on account of the battery. Otherwise we poison the earth."

"Don't forget to double-wrap it in black plastic before you drop it in the Dumpster. They won't take it otherwise." I left him to his work and climbed the stairway to the stars.

I'd met the former tenant in passing. I remembered a haircut resembling a mushroom cap, two Twizzlers in a shirt pocket, and three sets of eyeglasses strung around his neck: one for the computer screen, another to read printouts, the third to find the other two. A few weeks after he'd left, a detective with the state police came around asking if he'd left a forwarding. Lansing suspected him of downloading child porn and selling it to habitual offenders who'd grown wary of cyberspace. It was that kind of building; not that you could blame a pile of brick for what took place within it. One of my neighbors had been in the Peace Corps. She probably had an FBI file nearly as thick as mine.

But that morning I thought about my three clients: one dead, another unaccounted for, the third busy lecturing professional spokesmen on how to reel in dangling participles. Oddly enough, I felt loyalty in direct reverse ratio to the monetary reward. The late Carl Fannon's fifteen hundred bucks ran third behind Emil Haas's twenty and Gwendolyn Haas's nothing. If I worked things right, I could satisfy them all in one swing of the sword: Zorro minus the horse and wardrobe.

If I worked things right.

As it turned out, to no one's surprise, least of all my own, they didn't. But I'm not a plumber or an electrician. They guarantee their work.

In a little while I dragged over the phone and pecked out a number from the pad on my desk. Three rings gave me a menu. The one I wanted gave me reception, and a cool voice I'd heard before that asked me to hold and didn't wait to see if I was okay with that. While I was waiting I took a drink, dealt myself a Winston, and bought myself a misdemeanor at the head of a match. I was blowing it out when the voice came back. I asked for Brita.

"She's on another line at the moment. May I ask who's calling?"

"Amos Walker. She'll remember me. She referred another party to me just this morning."

"Is it in connection with real estate?"

"About three hundred cubic feet." That would be the total of the dimensions of the vault in the Sentinel.

The line went dead. I waited for the click and a dial tone before making another try. Then a fresh voice came on, with a tone I associated with tall summer drinks.

"Who is calling?"

"Do you always do business this way? If the girl didn't give you my name, you should fire her. If you're just stalling for time, you should quit. I'll thank you and so will the firm."

A little gulp of silence that might have been a gasp; or more likely the party on the other end of the line repositioning its forces. "Yes, Mr. Walker; I remember you now. You have to understand we do business with a great many people in one day. I can't be expected—"

"Carl Fannon, please."

"I'm afraid he's away on business. Can I—"

"You can't. I'd like a chunk of your time when you can spare it."

"*My* time? But—"

"Don't be so modest. With one partner on the other side of the world and the other dropped off its edge, you're Velocity Financing. You know Fannon hired me and why. I've come into some information and I need to discuss how to handle it. That makes you the chosen one while he's walking on the Great Wall."

There was a brief cool silence on her end. Then: "May I finish a sentence now?"

"Knock yourself out."

"If you knew all the time he was in China, why did you ask to speak to him?"

"I'm collecting business excuses for a book I'm writing. I wanted to see how you'd play it."

"And your conclusion?"

"Meh."

Something rattled; probably keys on a device rather than a Rolodex. I hadn't evolved even that far; what numbers I didn't keep in my head I recorded in a little memorandum book and locked it in the safe.

The rattling stopped. "I can give you between eleven and eleven-fifteen this morning. There's a staff meeting at noon I'll have to prepare for."

"A half hour would be better."

"I'm afraid that's impossible."

"Ink me in then. One thing."

"I'm listening."

"Tell the staff you might be fifteen minutes late." I cradled the receiver.

EIGHT

The Parker Block is a single building sticking up six stories above Woodward Avenue, Detroit's main drag. It's been there more than 130 years, resting solidly on a cast-iron ground-floor front with arched windows above the fourth floor and gulls prowling the ledges for handouts. Copper letters mounted on the black-painted iron spell out B. SIEGEL CO. in relief. Siegel was one of the merchant princes of the Victorian era who invented the modern department store. Years ago they tore out the hanging cashier's cage inside and the system of ropes and pulleys that carried paper currency up and change back down, replaced the hydraulic lift system with electric motors, and erected partitions between Foundation Garments and Sporting Goods to rent them out as offices. It was the only property associated with Velocity it didn't own, either alone or on behalf of a foreign backer; there are still some places around that aren't for sale. The company had settled for the top two floors and a whopping tax break from City Hall.

The elevator I rode no longer had a folding cage, but the

original bronze-finish doors were intact and the back wall mirrored for no reason I could figure apart from a last-ditch opportunity to straighten one's tie or adjust one's girdle before yakking with someone upstairs. My tie was straight, suit pressed, shoes shined. I wore them for the first time. The old pair had gone out with the trash. They'd left tracks in the dust on the floor of the vault. Intaglio marks, fingerprints, and bits of clay are still meat to the forensics team even in the age of DNA. I still hadn't made up my mind about whether I'd report what I'd found to the authorities. That was part of the reason I'd made this appointment.

The secret was still exclusive, apparently. I hadn't passed any blue-and-whites parked in front of the Sentinel Building on my way there. On the other hand, there might be a squad of uniforms camped out inside waiting for the criminal to return to the scene of the crime, corny as it sounds. Corny is one thing cops don't mind being called.

The doors glided open opposite a wall of tinted glass with the hollow *V* in the company's name outracing the other letters etched on it in gold. Beneath it:

EMIL HAAS, C.E.O.
CARL FANNON, President

I'd always thought they were the same thing. I had a lot to learn about business: like how to make it pay.

I used a glass handle and slogged through mint-green carpet to another sheet of glass on thin legs and a pair of human legs between them that hadn't much more heft. The woman who owned them lowered her magazine, marking her place with a finger, and smiled. She was as thin as her legs. Her cheekbones were painfully obvious and the flat planes of her skull showed under a fringe of glossy black hair. Fannon must have recruited her from the floor of the North American Auto Show in Cobo Hall. Only professional models and concentration camp survivors can be that skinny and live.

"Yes, Mr. Walker," she said when I gave her my card. "Mrs. Palmerston is engaged at present, but if you'll have a seat she'll come out presently."

"Nice vocabulary. Who drilled you, Emil or Gwendolyn?"

Her smile was skeletal. "*Reader's Digest.*" She held up the copy she'd been reading. "Have you ever met a middle-aged receptionist?"

"No, come to think of it."

"They all marry moles in cubicles and retire. Except this one. She's breaking the chain."

I gave her another card. "For you. Remember me when you pass the Bar."

Smiling, she tucked it inside the back cover and went back to reading.

In the reception room a black leather director's chair put my legs to sleep in five minutes. I got up, watched a plant eat a fly in a brass birdcage big enough to hold a go-go dancer, and inspected the wall art.

Blow-ups showcased spectacular old local buildings long since gone to wrecking bars and dynamite: the La Salle Hotel, J. L. Hudson's, the Packard Plant, the original Pontchartrain—which in the impatience of 1920s progress the city had torn down just thirteen years after it was erected, the Olympia Stadium, a lot of structures from before even my grandfather's time that looked like chandeliers and

French pastry. The subliminal message was that had Velocity been up and running then, all those treasures would have been spared.

Or maybe the pictures had come with one of its acquisitions, and the frames happened to match the molding. The trouble with being a detective is everything has to mean something. I sat back down.

Miss Thin Mints seemed to find something of interest on every page of her magazine, even the Rosetta ads; but had turned over the back cover with a sigh and directed her attention to the finish on her nails when something buzzed. She didn't pick up a receiver or flip a switch that I saw, just touched a button in one ear and handed me another of her ghastly smiles. "Mrs. Palmerston will be right out."

"Thank you so much." I wanted to ask if I should rise or touch the floor with my forehead. That rug could choke a porpoise.

"Mr. Walker? Brita Palmerston. I run the joint."

She wasn't any taller than she had to be, but the monochrome business suit—black, with golden threads running through it—and modest heels gave the impression of female gigantism; I was a little surprised when I got up from my iron maiden and her forehead came just to the bridge of my nose. She had brown hair with coppery highlights she didn't need. What's wrong with plain brown? I associated it with good furniture, a stream brimming with trout, mellow whisky, and dark chocolate. I bet when she took out all the pins and let it go it would fall as far as her shoulder blades. The figure was good, the calves muscular where the hem of the skirt caught them, but not so much I didn't think I could take her at Indian wrestling. I couldn't tell if she wore hose or tanning lotion on bare legs. Something about her apart from the cool long pour of her businesslike demeanor made me want to take her shoes off and find out for myself.

Then again, all that might just have been part of the front the place put up. As many civilizations had been built on sex appeal as had been brought down by them.

"You have gray eyes," I said.

"I didn't mean to. Is that bad?"

"Just unusual. They don't pass them out with brown hair every day."

"Yours are hazel—I think. Darker." She stepped closer. I felt her body heat before I smelled the light scent she wore.

"No; it's the whites. They're a bit cloudy."

"Mysterious, you mean. Burst vessels. Case closed."

I grinned. After a beat, she did, too; if you could call the three inches of teeth she measured out anything so work-inappropriate. "Since this is about Mr. Fannon, perhaps we should use his office."

"Yes, let's. We can compare square footage."

I followed her, and her scent, down a broad two-toned hallway plastered with more extinct architecture and through an unmarked door into a two-story flat outfitted for business. Width-wise it wasn't any bigger than it had to be, but as for tall a working farmer would look at it and think in terms of silage, with sunshine tinkling through a stained-glass skylight at the top.

Someone had pierced the ceiling to endow a library in the top-floor office that had separated this one from the skylight. A freestanding spiral staircase—an engineering marvel in itself, independent of the law of gravity—led to shelves of tall books with the names of celebrated architects, extinct also, lettered vertically on the metallic jackets. Under this canopy stood a Spanish galleon of a desk, a five-thousand-dollar showpiece in any upscale antiques shop, with claw-and-ball feet; a design I could never understand. Raptors have better things to do than play ball, such as swoop down on small unsuspecting rodents and tear them to pieces. One of the claws was ingrown and swollen. The featherweight computer monitor on the green leather blotter went with that piece of history like a spaceship in Queen Victoria's dollhouse. All the keys on a combination intercom and telephone were blinking fit to bust.

A lot of people wanted to get in touch with Carl Fannon. A lot of people were in for a winter of discontent; but for the moment I was the only one in possession of that gem. If I were financially astute I'd have sold out all my stock in Velocity Financing before the run. But if I were financially astute, I'd have owned some.

The walls were paneled and hung with Renaissance prints in rich colors of titled frog-eyed characters with combs in their hair and lace cuffs, the men clawing away at enormous world globes and the women clutching small slim volumes of poetry bound in red leather. Guess which had steered the course of history?

Brita Palmerston caught me admiring them. "Mr. Fannon commissioned the photos. He owns the originals; but of course you can't hang a half-million in oils in a place of business. The insurance company would never stand for it."

"He probably keeps them in a vault."

I didn't stress the last word: I wasn't a player on stage, with the cheap seats at the back to consider. I pretended to study a portrait of a girl in a Bo Peep bonnet carrying a

basket of flowers, but I could have saved myself the subter-
fuge. Brita shrugged a disinterested shrug. "No doubt.
Personally, if I were to spend my hard-earned money on
something frivolous, I'd want to show it off."

"I don't suppose Mr. Palmerston would object to that."

When I turned to face her, there was no evidence that a
smile could have fed off that face. "My father was killed in
the first Gulf War."

"So sorry, on two counts. I thought the 'Mrs.' was sig-
nificant."

"My ex-husband went by another name. But when you go
back to Miss, the wolves slink out from every crack and
hole." She raised her left hand, ostensibly to push back a
stray lock of brown hair. A thin gold band with a small diamond glittered on the usual finger.

"The sexes aren't so hard to sort out," I said. "You just
have to think of yourself and go opposite. Men slip off their
wedding rings and stick them in a pocket. Women brandish
them like a forty-five."

Her smile this time was more measured still, the lips tight.
"Enough about me, Mr. Walker. Let's talk about you."

NINE

There isn't much to tell," I said. "Most of it's on the card I gave the receptionist."

"You can get only so much on a card. These days, you need both sides just to list all the contact numbers. Here at Velocity we like to know a bit more about the people we do business with than just how to get in touch with them."

We were sitting facing each other across the desk, which put us as far apart as the doomed American Indian lovers standing on opposite shores of Gitche Gumee. The padded number I sat in was comfortable, but the legs were just short enough to give her the high ground, resting her lovely hands on the arms of a winged tufted-leather chair that almost swallowed her; although if it had tried I had the distinct impression it would be like a bear trying to choke down a porcupine backwards. Just on our brief acquaintance I knew as much about her as I'd spilled about myself. I crossed my legs.

"I'm a private investigator, licensed by the State of Michigan, bottled in bond. I have been since whales had feet.

I'm past middle age, but there should be a designation between it and geezer, like 'young adult' between teenage punk
and mature stuffed shirt. I've been in jail a couple of times—
okay, four, if you count three hours in holding, which is like
dog years if you've ever experienced it. I doubt you have. I've
been shot at, hit twice; the last is still with me and always
will be, especially when I don't live right, which I don't as a
rule. I have some impressive references, but I don't like to
bother them with just anyone calling to verify; otherwise I
won't have them long. I fought for my country, if that means
anything these days, and I spent just long enough training
for police duty to realize I didn't belong there. The police
agreed. I was married once, but you've been there, so I doubt
I need go into that."

"That's one piece of personal information I wish I'd kept
to myself. Tell me something else."

"I once saw Frank Sinatra walking through Cadillac
Square with his bodyguards. He was taller than I thought."

"Something I'd care to know."

"That's the shebang, unless you want to see some scars."

She passed on that, a bit to my disappointment. "Now
that we're on such intimate terms, tell me what you came to
tell Mr. Fannon. Let's not have any nonsense about confidentiality. I run this office. We can't all be geniuses or media
whores. Someone has to keep track of paper clips and bank
deposits. I'm the one who suggested he consult you about
Mr. Haas's disappearance. Have you made any progress in
finding him?"

"No," I said truthfully. If she'd asked if Mr. Haas had
found me before I'd begun looking for him, the answer
would have been the same, with no truth in it at all. She

wasn't my client. Just then I was carrying so many on my back, one more would put me in traction. "I just wanted to bring Fannon up to speed on all the places I've looked where Haas isn't."

"I hardly think that would be helpful. Negative information is no information at all."

"Not so. It takes an honest P.I. to separate negative from positive. The schemers run out that process as far as they can, going over old ground and burning the client's money. In any case, I'd rather hear it from him. In a pure business sense, Fannon knows Haas better than anyone. Since we spoke yesterday morning, he's had more time to think about where else I might look."

"Are you suggesting he held out on you the first time?"

"Not intentionally. It's like when you've had a break-in. In the heat of the moment you call the cops and report what was taken. Then when you've had a chance to cool down you start to notice some other things you missed missing the first time. If it's your class ring from the University of De-troit, that's something for the insurance company, nobody else. If, say, it's a file on an employee you let go who might hold a grudge, that's just the kind of thing a good missing-persons investigator can get his teeth into.

"Something like that," I added. "I'd rather hear it from him. I've no reason to think a benevolent boss like Carl Fan-non would have soiled his hands with something so trivial. I'm just opening a new avenue of pursuit."

"You think cutting off someone's sole support a trivial matter?"

I'd crossed my legs one direction. Now I crossed them in the other. "Let's leave management-versus-labor to the folk-singing circuit. Gray matter has a way of spilling over to form gray eyes. You're intelligent enough to know a hypothetical observation when you hear it. Anyone can overlook something important when he thinks it's not connected to the matter at hand. It's my job to see if there's a connection, or if there isn't, to run the thing down and eliminate it. I'd rather hear it from him."

"Do you have to keep saying that?"

"Until I hear from him."

The monitor on the desk chimed. I might have dismissed it as white noise, the kind of ambient music that scores any office in the twenty-first century, if I hadn't heard the identical notes coming from Carl Fannon's wrist-mounted Eniac. A pair of gray eyes flicked toward the monitor, narrowed, smoothed out. She sat back, rubbing the back of one lovely hand with the other. If I had a week to spare I'd have had all her tells in inventory—and probably known no more about what was behind them than I knew at that moment.

"I'm afraid we're talking in circles, Mr. Walker. Until Mr. Fannon's plane touches down and I can reach him—notwithstanding the time spent collecting his luggage and finding transportation to his hotel, and the dozen or so calls he'll place en route—we can go no further."

I recrossed my legs. Having a hole card is no good unless you know when to play it. I took a chance.

"What makes you so sure he's in China?"

"It's a long flight by any standards, with any number of possible delays. I can't be certain he's there until he touches base."

To hell with it. I began laying out my hand.

"I imagine he'll do that as soon as he gets the text you sent him."

Three thin creases etched themselves against her perfect brow. "What text are you talking about?"

I'd been called; the time had come to spread out my cards. I uncrossed my legs, drew my notepad from my inside breast pocket, turned it to the page I'd written on most recently, and showed it to her.

Brita Palmerston didn't move her lips when she read. If she had, I'd have given up my last shred of faith in whatever instincts I'd developed in the course of my calling. But I followed a pair of gray eyes as they read the lines I'd copied from the screen on the face of Carl Fannon's wristwatch. Nothing of shattering import, in the text itself; just the text itself:

CALL C.F. THE MOMENT YOU LAND.

BP

I said, "C.F. is Cecil Fish, I assume. He's the worm in Velocity's salad. He'd be a worm even without the greens. I'm assuming the other set of initials belongs to you; unless Fannon's interested in acquiring British Petroleum."

I sat back as it sank in, flipping shut my pad. I felt like Kreskin, only without the sense of triumph. On further consideration, I felt like a state trooper informing a worried mother he'd just unwrapped her teenage son from around a light pole on I-94.

TEN

How could you have come by that text?" she asked. "I sent it yesterday, just before closing. We spend a lot of money securing our communications from the outside."

"It isn't wasted," I said, "so far as I can tell. I scooped up the communication from where it was addressed.

"He didn't make it to China," I added. "He didn't make it ten blocks from where we're sitting. Unless the cops are more on the ball and more subtle about it than usual, he's lying where I last saw him, collecting dust in a vault in the basement of the Sentinel Building."

Somewhere in the world a butterfly landed on a tasty blossom. In downtown Detroit a scrap of understanding drifted onto an office manager.

"Are you saying Carl Fannon's dead?"

"He was as of last night, in the old bank vault in the basement of the Sentinel Building. I won't go into the details of how I happened to find him there; that's official business, as soon as the officials catch up to me. Either he got careless or someone helped him. I don't guess it matters to a man who choked to death."

She moved then, placing a well-kept hand to her own throat. "You're wrong. He's in China."

"If you say so. Meanwhile we've got the business of how I came by this text."

She rearranged the gewgaws on the desk, squaring the green marble pen set with the edge of the blotter, placing the stainless steel letter opener where Fannon's hand would come to rest on it when it was needed, all these things done with the efficiency of an undertaker attending to the bereaved.

"The things we do when we don't know what to say," I said. "He's beyond caring how his stuff is arranged."

She smacked her hands on the desktop. "You didn't know him. If I weren't here to organize things, any potential investor would take one look at the rat's nest where he worked and leave by the next available elevator." She raised a hand to each temple, massaging it in circular motions. "Work*s*, I mean; present tense. Now you've got me doing it."

"I've got you believing it. I thought I'd have to go back and take a picture. I doubt it would make it into one of the swanky magazines in your reception area, but it might convince you your boss is dead. *Todt. Muerto. Mort. Nekros.* No pulse. D-E-A-D." I spelled it out in sign language. "You know something? With people like you pulling for him he might snap out of it yet."

"You're taking a chance, Walker. If there's been a murder and you knew about it and didn't report it, you could be in for a laundry list of criminal charges."

"I already am, if the cops think knowing about it twenty-four hours after the fact would do a damn thing toward clearing it up. This wasn't a fatal carjacking, with some junkie gangbanger spraying clues all over the room like a tomcat. One of the reasons I came here was to pin you down as a suspect or eliminate you entirely. On brief acquaintance I don't think Nick the Greek would expect you to foam at the mouth and throw this desk at me when I dropped the word 'vault' into the conversation. He played poker with his opponents' faces, not cards. That's one down, less than a million to go. If the thing spreads outside the city limits, I'm going to have to farm it out; but at least I've dealt you out of the deck. I'd say that's a fair day's work."

"Isn't that for the police to determine? Assuming you're not making all this up just to wangle another fat retainer. The last I heard, private detectives didn't investigate murder."

"They do when they keep tripping over them. Maybe it's my destiny, but there are days when I can't take a stroll downtown without stubbing my toe on a cadaver."

"Then isn't it your duty as a citizen to hand it over to the people who are paid to find out how the cadaver became a cadaver?"

I dealt myself a cigarette, just to see if she rose to the assault on state law. She took it like the Berlin Wall took spray paint; from the western side. I didn't light it. "As you implied, I'm carrying some of Fannon's fat retainer on my hip. The rest is in the bank. I'd like to earn it. I'm too poor to go around giving refunds."

"I processed that check, as part of my responsibilities to this firm. It was given you to find Emil Haas. Have you found him?"

"Not yet," I said; again truthfully. I'd been walking a tightrope so long I ought to have qualified for a patent. "That's the other reason I'm here. Has he turned up?"

"No. Have you spoken to his daughter?"

"She spoke to me. I had a busy day yesterday," I said, walking the cigarette across the back of one hand. Her eyes followed it the way a dog follows any movement preceding a treat. "I've a hunch today will be no different. He was supposed to meet me last night in the basement of the Sentinel Building."

She flattened her palms on the desk again, this time without the sound of a pistol report. "You've *seen* him? But you said—Just a moment." She reached under the desk.

Something whirred and a section of paneling behind the desk slid into a pocket, exposing a lot of glass, crystal, and stainless steel. She got up, opened a dwarf refrigerator under the sink, tonged three ice cubes into each of a pair of thick-bottomed glasses, and filled them with golden liquid from a square bottle with a foil label. She came back, set one of the glasses in front of me, and sat back in the executive seat holding the other in both hands.

"I'm assuming you have no objections to Scotch."

"I lost that fight in college," I said. "Back then, if you didn't have a glass in your hand, it was a mortal insult to your host. So I asked for Scotch, a drink I could nurse all night. The joke was on me. I discovered a taste for it." I leaned forward to touch glasses, straining my arm with the effort. It was one hell of a desk. The stuff tasted like fermented honey filtered through Harris Tweed.

"A college man," she said. "Who'd've thought?"

"Those days they let everybody in. Let's take up where

we left off. I said I hadn't found Haas. He found me, and paid me another fat retainer—fat in the sense that twenty bucks is fat to a homeless person who lives on hot dogs." I didn't know why the drifter I'd treated to a package of wieners had popped into my head at just that moment; Frank, that was the name. "I took only that much even though he wanted to give me my standard advance."

"Fifteen hundred dollars," she said. "Five hundred dollars a day. That's twenty-five hundred a week."

"Since you're so good at math, figure out what that comes to when I work six weeks in a year."

She totaled it in an instant. "I'm still listening."

"Depending on what he intended to tell me in the basement I might have collected the rest. He didn't show. Fannon did, but as indicated previously, he wasn't very helpful."

She took a second sip, set down her glass, and lifted the receiver off the pinball machine at her elbow. "I think the rest of this conversation should involve the police."

"I agree." I stuck out my free hand and waggled the fingers. After an instant's hesitation she pressed an unlighted key and handed the receiver to me. I pressed star nine-sixty-seven, canceling out the source of the call, and dialed three digits.

"Nine-one-one. What is your emergency?"

"Inspector Alderdyce, please. I want to report a homicide."

The female operator spoke as if someone had forgotten to turn off the iron in someone's apartment. "Your name, sir?"

"Amos Walker."

"Spell it, please."

"D.O.A."

I handed back the receiver for her to cradle.

Her hand rested on it. "What do I tell them when they come to call?"

"Your life story, if you want. Nothing if you don't. You don't know anything. In fact I was never here." I got up.

She tilted Carl Fannon's chair forward, splaying her hands on the desk. She seemed altogether too comfortable in that office; but that was just the detective in me, always suspecting everything of everyone. In a few months I'd be accusing the Easter bunny of keeping a hen on the side.

"If you're expecting me to cover for you—" she said.

"Nothing of the sort. Just trying to keep things less complicated for the cops. Good morning, Mrs. Palmerston. You know how to get in touch with me if you want."

Inspector John Alderdyce, my go-to cop whenever I find a human being lounging around at room temperature, was on vacation, fishing for salmon in Alaska. The lap the case fell into was a lieutenant named Child; although if he'd ever been one he showed no indication when he came in and plunked himself down in the customer's chair. He was about a yard wide across the shoulders and just over the minimum height for police duty. His head was built to scale; hatting it would be a challenge, so he didn't. He had a nice growth of black hair striped with gray and took care of it. Fresh clippings were pasted to his shirt collar with something like bay rum. His face was too small for his head, with all the features crowded into the middle.

I didn't know him. I figured he'd transferred over from another division, possibly the gang squad. The new chief had disbanded it recently; not because the gang situation had improved, but because the press could no longer tell the difference between the opposing sides. That's how it was in guerrilla warfare, which is what the streets of our city became after sundown.

"Honest folks generally hang around when they come on a dead body." His voice was shallow for his age—I put him a year or two past his twenty—and very, very gentle. I trusted that the way I trust a faith healer with a limp.

"Scared folks do," I said. "I go all to pieces over roadkill."

"Quick but not good. Try again."

I was acting professional as all hell, slitting open junk mail on the desk. Since his phone call came announcing he was coming to see me about a little murder I hadn't even lit a cigarette. It's against the law in a place of business in our state, and I was in trouble enough.

I laid aside the penknife. "Emil Haas, the dead man's partner, sat where you're sitting yesterday morning, asking me to meet him in the Sentinel basement that evening. I was there, he wasn't. Carl Fannon was. I wanted to talk to the office manager where he worked before reporting it, to see if I was the only one in on the secret."

"Were you?"

"So far as I could tell. If you've talked to Brita Palmerston, you know she rattles about as easy as a big-time crook on his fiftieth visit to police headquarters."

"I did. She didn't strike me as any kind of a crook at all."

"I didn't say she was. It was a simile."

"Three syllables. I guess you're not your garden-variety window peeper."

I looked at the card he'd given me: plain white stock, with

only his name and extension on the department line in black block. "'Childe Harold to the dark tower came,'" I said.

He bared his lower teeth in what I supposed he thought was a smile. "I get that sometimes. If my name was Lipschitz I wouldn't know any poetry at all. You won't get anywhere running on idle, Walker. No one ever does. That's why they call it stalling. A fragile little thing like a license can get busted over failing to report a homicide."

"Before that happened I'd have to put on a clean shirt and drive clear up to Lansing and face the board. Don't waste time telling me you don't know in what high regard those state troopers hold a city cop."

"Go ahead, be a schmuck. It wouldn't be *my* first choice when a city cop's got me dead to rights, but the world's full of characters."

I parked his card under my phone. No telling when I'd need a friend on the force. "Why don't let's tear up the declaration of war and start over from scratch?"

"Too late, Jim. Something over eighteen hours too late. That's the jump we'd've had on whoever it was forgot he had a rich multimillionaire on ice and left him gasping."

"I had this conversation with Fannon's office manager. The upshot was our absent-minded friend was long gone on the red-eye to Vegas or anywhere else when I opened that door. If this is a pinch, let's have it. I'm out of work anyway, and it's corned beef hash night at County. Your superior sent the chef up himself, straight from the four-star restaurant where he worked."

He looked at the Bulova strapped to the underside of his wrist; I don't trust men who wear their watches that way. It's too easy to sneak a look at the time when you're boring them to death. "I was wondering just how long it would take you to draw the Alderdyce card. I know you're tight. Somehow I think you're still loose enough for me to call that bluff."

A good man with words, Lieutenant Child. I had the impression he'd read more of Byron than he let on.

ELEVEN

'm only tough when I have to be," Child said. "It ages you. You know what's behind me and what it can do if you think you can outsmart it."

I said, "If I were that smart I wouldn't be working this job. The system's Bugs Bunny. I'm strictly Elmer Fudd."

"Bugs is clever. We're not. We're just there. All the time, day and night, weekends and Christmas. We'll wear you down like a river running through rock."

My smile tasted bitter. "G'wan with you, Lieutenant. You're a poet after all. I only mentioned Alderdyce to keep the conversation going. If I thought my past associations put a thumb on your scale, it would mean I haven't learned anything about the police in thirty years. If this were the Middle Ages you'd each be forted up behind a stone fence with your own personal moat. You don't break cases by avoiding stepping on the toes of your brothers in blue."

"You got me wrong, Walker. I'm not an ambitious man. But every now and then I got to break one just to show I'm not just drifting toward retirement. A thing like that can get you canned just before your pension's ready to kick in. I got just enough ambition to want to prevent that. Any idea what Haas wanted to talk to you about and why not here?"

"No on both counts."

"Guess."

"Uh-uh. The *G* in that one stands for gullible. If it turns out to be wrong, a by-the-book type like you could blow it up into lying to a cop."

"I'm not that hard to get along with. It's just this face. Tell it like you heard it from somebody else."

"Okay. Just on a hunch I'd say he's nervous about this Sentinel Building deal, or maybe he's been nervous about what he and Fannon have been doing for some time and it's just the straw that broke the yak's back. Not knowing this dump, he couldn't be sure no one might be listening in, so he chose a deep dark place with unbroken concrete walls."

"What's a plutocrat like him got to be nervous about? Money can buy everything. Don't let 'em tell you any different. Ask the man who hasn't any."

"Like I've got another office on Lake Shore Drive. I only keep this one to fool people into thinking I'm honest. What's he got to be nervous about? How he makes his money, to begin with. If the last few years have taught us nothing else, they've taught us that all those piles of cash a man's got salted away can vanish like a slug in the sun once the feds open a file on him. You know Cecil Fish?"

The crowded features pinched closer together yet. "We met when he was the city prosecutor in Iroquois Heights, before they busted him. I hear he's some kind of paid lobbyist now. Crooked politicians are like black locust. Chop one down and he sprouts back up from the stump."

"He's been making noise about Velocity Financing fronting for foreign interests when it acquires property in Detroit. That's a big stink to hang under the public's nose, 'foreign interests.' Could be China or Portugal or those maniacs in turbans who think they invented decapitation. It wouldn't work in Europe, where they live cheek-by-jowl, but here it's a popular phobia. So far he hasn't proof or he'd have swung it by now, but it could be the talk has got Haas worrying too much because his partner doesn't worry enough."

I waited while he looked at that from all sides. Down in the street a sanitation truck scooped up a Dumpster with a bang they heard in Baghdad. Finally he spoke.

"That's pretty specific for a stab in the dark."

"Still that's all it is."

"I wonder."

Cops. Tell them the truth straight out and they never appreciate it. They like it better when you try out a couple of lies on them first. If this one was a priest he'd grill you for an hour before giving Last Rites.

"Okay," I said, "I'll take another couple of swipes. Fannon found out Haas was going behind his back, rigged up that trip to Beijing as an alibi intending to eliminate him, and Haas turned the tables. That would mean there was something to Fish's accusation. Or Haas intended for Fannon to find out about our meeting so he could lure him into that vault. Was I right about cause of death, suffocation?"

"At a glance, unless he used purple nail polish. Of course, we'll have to wait till the lab monkeys tell us what we already know, with some pig Latin thrown in." He blew a gust of air. "I've been in this racket too long. The CID used to own the crime scene. Now we have to stand around with our thumbs up our asses while some fresh punk in paper shoes goes over the place with a black light, and in the end what do we know? As much as we did just in the door. In ten years we'll all be coming to work with stethoscopes instead of guns and wearing scrubs over our Kevlar. Not me, though. I'll be fresh retired, if they don't bounce me first."

His exhaustion was contagious. I'd have felt like retiring myself, if I didn't know that dead-dog weariness for a cop ploy, older even than that Jekyll-and-Hyde routine they played out in interrogation. *Brother, I'm so far gone I wouldn't hear you even if you confessed to killing Hoffa.* Five minutes after he left my office he'd be tap-dancing down the street whistling Gilbert and Sullivan.

I said, "If I'm right about the murderer and the motive, it would mean Haas had the proof Fish hasn't."

"Why drag you into it at all?"

"Whoever shut that door fixed the time lock to open it just after I arrived for our appointment. Maybe Haas wanted to implicate me somehow to draw lightning away from him. And maybe that's why I made with the feet so I could wrap the whole thing up in Christmas paper with a fat bow, just like Nero Wolfe, before my license got bent."

It was his turn to shake his head. "It all fits the facts, but there are holes in it you could drive a bus through. Airlines these days are more careful than ever about checking the manifest. They'd know Fannon missed that plane before it got off the ground. The guy logged enough frequent-flyer hours to know that. The rest is just hot air—except the part about you getting scared and rabbiting the scene. That part's as solid as that vault."

A set of nicotine-stained fingers fumbled a crumpled package of Pall Mall straight-ends out of an inside pocket. I waited until he fired one up off a throwaway butane lighter, then struck a match and put it to one of my own. We sat breaking the law for a couple of minutes, then he shot twin gray jets out of his tiny nostrils and planted his hands on the arms of the chair. The cigarette went on smoldering in a notch in his lower lip.

"It goes way against the grain, but since you're the last person I know for sure laid eyes on Emil Haas, you won't make much good bait eating County hash for forgetting your civic responsibilities. You're no killer, that much I know about the people Alderdyce chooses to hang with. I'll tell the chief you took fright, then on reflection decided to make an honest citizen out of yourself and made the call. He'll chew my ass off, but if there's the smallest chance Haas creeps out of his corner to do over that meeting, we need you out in the open where he can get to you."

He levered himself to his feet, seemed to realize he too was smoking, snatched the butt loose, and flung it in a corner, where it burned a new crater in the linoleum. "If he does show, don't be shy this time."

"I won't. All right if I do a little poking around myself?"

He stood with his suitcoat hanging open and the checked butt of a semiautomatic in cross-draw position in a clip on his belt. God, he looked beat; I almost offered him a lie-down on the bench in my waiting room. "Depends on where you poke and what you poke it with."

"I'd like to pay a call on Fish. We met more than once.

We can discuss old times and maybe I can find out if he's holding a full house or just a fistful of feathers."

"What's the percentage? Your client's dead."

I didn't tell him I had two others, one who'd bought me cheap, the other strictly honorary. He hadn't thought to ask about Gwendolyn Haas.

In a pig's eye he hadn't. I was supposed to walk the high wire waiting for that particular shoe to drop. No, Lieutenant Child didn't like being tough. Neither does a grizzly. He just is, and he's patient enough to wait for his opening.

But that clean I wasn't ready to come just yet. "Fannon paid me to find Haas. If Fish has anything, it might flush him out and I can spend the retainer without looking away, like a guy cheating himself at solitaire."

He took a comb from his shirt pocket, but he didn't comb his hair. He tapped it against the palm of his other hand. "Honest Abe, that's you. I bet when you were a kid you hiked ten miles to return a book." He put away the comb, noticed his coat was open, and buttoned it with a shrug. "Anything to spare me five minutes with that kisser. Don't forget to tell a guy what you find out; even if it's nothing but feathers. I only make new mistakes. Never the same one twice."

He left. I got up, picked up the butt, and laid it in the ashtray to smoke itself out. Under the smear of ash was a picture of Traverse City. I tried to remember the details of when I'd been there. It seemed to me I was in trouble that time too.

TWELVE

My watch said it was still morning. I scowled at the second hand, but it was moving. That was two days in a row I'd crammed what seemed like a full day's work into a couple of hours. The smart thing to do was to call it that and go home and rest up for what came next. It was so smart I looked up the number of Cecil Fish's consulting firm in Iroquois Heights and dialed it.

I got an eager-sounding male legal secretary or something who told me Mr. Fish was in a meeting. That was okay with me. I said, "When he's free, I've got something he'll want to hear."

"Mr. Fish no longer practices law; but if it's legal advice you want, we have several attorneys on staff."

It was a genteel way of confirming his boss had been disbarred for life.

I made my voice gruff. It was getting easier to do by the day. I twisted out the butt I'd lit off the stub of the last. "I got all the advice I need. But if he wants to know who's been bankrolling Fannon and Haas, he'll see me."

"Your name?"

"Frank Wiener." I filled the brief pause on his end. "I'm kidded about it a lot. My parents wanted a girl."

"Hold, please."

The line went silent; or so I thought. After a couple of seconds Ravel's *Bolero* began to surface, as timidly as a novice nurse knocking on the door to ask if you were undressed yet. The notes were becoming louder and more insistent when the voice came back on. "Thanks for holding, Mr. Wiener. Mr. Fish will see you today at two o'clock."

That gave me time for lunch. An English-type pub had moved into the abandoned service station across from my office, with colored pennants flapping and a GRAND OPENING banner across the faux stone façade. I drank a beer and ate a cheese sandwich deep-fried in crankcase oil. There were darts stuck in a corkboard target in too-random order and the bartender wore a Union Jack vest and a black bow tie. In another week he'd break out the monocle. If he was still working then. Judging by the droves who weren't fighting to get in I gave the place six weeks tops.

It was a shame. The same radio station that had interviewed Carl Fannon had given it the big buildup, with free nachos for the staff. I decided they worked for food.

For all its ambitions toward Evelyn Waugh the place had conceded to the twenty-first century and installed a big-screen TV, but with the sound turned down. There was a shot of Carl Fannon's hand-lasted shoes poking out from under a sheet on a gurney wheeling out of the Sentinel Building, cutting to an earnest female face sweating through pancake with a microphone held to her mouth and nothing coming out. It was as good a way as any to cover an atrocity; better than most. I hoped it would catch on. My name didn't appear, either in the banner rolling across the bottom of the screen or on the woman's lips.

"Killer Unknown" joined the parade of letters sliding from right to left. That summed it up. The footage was just filler.

Killers. I'd become an expert on the type, purely by accident. I was a divining rod for locating stiffs, a compass whose needle always pointed six feet down, the human counterpart of a carcass-sniffing dog. I knew the people who supplied victims by species and subspecies, and at what point a subspecies acquired enough characteristics of its own to upgrade to species: the Darwin of Death. There were goons who stuck a gun at you while you were gassing up, just for your ride, and almost as an afterthought put one through your liver on their way from the curb. There were nail-biters who slew out of anger or rage or fear — "Raskolnikovs," the cops who read called them. So many killed for personal gain they were filed by variety: the bank robber who shot his way out with his bag of dye packets, the nephew with gambling debts who helped his rich aunt downstairs with a shove, the wino who slew a fellow traveler over two swallows of Thunderbird. Sex killers, thrill killers, killers who should have murdered their abominable mothers when it counted, and spared the lives of dozens of women who resembled them in some way; mercy killers, pulling the plug on golden-anniversary spouses to spare them the long agony of terminal disease; and let's not forget Kevorkian, a retired corpse-cutter so obsessed with death he painted grisly graveyard scenes and helped dozens of sufferers through the gate and got commended for it by the kind of doctrinarian who devalued life in the womb as well as in the wheelchair, but who was a glorified serial killer just the same. People who killed from boredom, to challenge authority, for fun, or on some sudden impulse, like squashing a bug going about its perfectly acceptable way in the grass at their feet. Revenge killers, looking to pay off an old grudge. Killers who killed to make a point: the mob thought they had the corner on that one, when some character ignored a warning or figured he was clever enough to steal from the no-necks because they couldn't go to the cops; but the cops themselves had a piece of that action, killing killers who'd killed one of their own; execution posing as a firefight, only with no cameras around to confirm either version.

Amateurs, most of them. Homicide is the one crime most often committed by first offenders. The majority are cuffed on the spot, standing over their victims holding the weapon. Others try to dress the scene to look like robbery or random savagery, forgetting or not knowing that the people who investigate murders are wise to all the tricks and sit back like Lieutenant Child, droopy-eyed and only paying half-attention to all the leaks in your story until they strike like lightning. Three-toed sloths are that way, they say on *When Animals Attack*: hanging from their tree limbs like wet laundry, moving their limbs slow as the hands of a clock until suddenly a fistful of claws the size of a platter swats off the left side of your face.

Then there are the remote-control killers. Their weapon is a phone, or maybe just a nod over a table in a restaurant.

Whitey Bulger was one of those. Eleven was the official count. In order to nail him the feds had let walk the man who actually got blood under his nails. I didn't know how I felt about that. Yes, I did; but I could see their point, even if I disagreed with it. The small percentage of killers with professional experience almost never see the inside of a cell block.

Finally there are the worst killers of all: the ones who get away. Every homicide dick fears them the way he fears being laid off with a house under construction and a wife pregnant with triplets. With that detective in mind, I overtipped the server and felt like a chump going out the door.

Now that the lot was occupied I'd had to garage the Cutlass a couple of blocks down Grand River. I never found out what happened to the vagrant who'd slept in the station before they gave him the boot. Unlike Frank, he hadn't been sociable enough to introduce himself, and I couldn't pay him off with lunchmeat. The fee the garage charged was only a little more than what he'd extorted to protect the car from vandals—him—but getting it now involved three extra flights of stairs lit by forty-watt bulbs. You shouldn't have to pack a revolver just to park your car in the Motor City.

Someone had sprayed green paint across the sign that read IROQUOIS HEIGHTS, HOME OF THE 1997 CHAMPION WARRIORS. There was a move on to change the high school team's name because it offended Native Americans. I understood they were going to expel Indiana from the Union for the same reason. That should finish the job Custer started.

The city council had reconfigured the central street along the zigzag lines of a drift fence and plopped a roundabout

smack in the middle of the main four corners just to increase
the likelihood of fender-benders and tickets for careless driving. It's that kind of place. Every few terms someone gets
into office on a reform platform, but in between it always
reverts to type. The bright storefronts and coach lamps are
pretty to look at; so is purple loosestrife, which chokes out
all the native vegetation and is just as ineradicable as the
kind of politician who used to tack down his tie with a diamond and smoke cigars with the band still on. I'd played a
walk-on role in putting one former mayor in jail and a larger
part in the mayhem that had destroyed the old downtown,
but that was old, old news.

Cecil Fish, once the city prosecutor, ran his image-
polishing firm in a part of the city I was unfamiliar with.
I was reading street signs when a sleek blue cruiser with a
five-pointed star stenciled on the side and on the hood
squished to a stop in a handicap spot and a deputy got out
and went into a tobacconist's, hauling up his gun belt. He'd
spend most of his day doing that because his belly would
keep pushing it down. Shortly after the voters turned the
old police headquarters into a sheriff's substation, the command officer in charge had enforced the county fitness re-
quirements, but that one got kicked under the radiator just
days after he quit. There would be a direct line in the back
of the smoke shop to the oddsmakers in Vegas and a little
something extra in the deputy's carton of Luckies. It's that
kind of place, until the population gets fed up again.

The building was a one-story ranch-type house with a
long covered porch like an old-time general store, but the
plate-glass display windows were masked by almond-colored

Venetian blinds, a shade lighter than the tan brick. On each window, lettered in white in an arc:

C. T. FISH CONSULTING

The earnest voice I'd encountered over the phone be-longed to a pudgy young feller in a J.C. Penney suit and a Trims R Us haircut whose big daily challenge seemed to be keeping his shirttail in his pants. I remembered being young; I'd been so for a long time, after all, but *earnest* was a long cast backwards into tangled reeds. The shirttail was still an issue, but I'd learned to look after that whenever I stood or slid out of a car seat.

"Yes, Mr. Wiener," he said, hauling out a portable phone to check the clock. "Right on time. All the way back, last door you come to."

I left him attending to his haberdashery and twenty-first-century pocket watch.

A beige hallway with nothing on the walls but a coat of oyster-colored paint ended in a door with all the features of a fire exit. Next to it on a plain steel panel was a red button like a poker chip. You just couldn't resist pushing it. A buzz, a click, and I stepped inside a large square room with a wres-tling mat on the floor and da Vinci's naked man spread-eagled in a circle on the wall facing the door. In the middle of this, Cecil Thutmose Fish stood in tennis whites swing-ing a racquet one-on-one against a pixilated opponent on a computer screen that covered the wall opposite. I couldn't tell who was ahead, but he played like someone who'd lost a set. The black-framed glasses he'd worn since seventh-grade debate class were fogged over and he'd stained his pale-blue sweats black. He spun on and kicked his two-hundred-dollar athletic shoes and grunted when he swung as if he were pitching a bale of hay from ground level into a loft.

He didn't know I was there. The world didn't exist while he was shadow-boxing Bobby Riggs in his prime. To me he looked like a man trying to put his pants on in a hurricane. If he were twenty years younger it would have been comical, but watching it made me wince for his brittle bones. Even Cecil Fish's bones. I'm not without pity.

He hadn't changed much. His blond hair, in bangs still, was graying when we'd met, but through a miracle of modern science it had gone all blond instead of the other way around. He'd had other work done as well, by someone who knew enough not to shrink-seal it in plastic, and what were probably regular workouts like today's had kept the flab away, but apart from thick tennis soles and lifts there wasn't anything he could do about being short.

I doubted he'd done anything about his main handicap. He wasn't bent in the usual sense of the term; if you offered him a briefcase full of unmarked bills he'd probably throw you out of his office, after calling in camera crews from all the local stations so the tree didn't fall unnoticed; but if you wrote a cashier's check made out to his political campaign, any union problems you might have would evaporate. I don't know if that laissez-faire attitude extended to brothels and horse parlors, but once you've grown accustomed to looking the other way you could get whiplash turning back. The only reason he wasn't pressing shirts in Club Fed was he'd had the good fortune to lose his son in an auto accident during jury selection. No honest prosecutor could out-box that.

I don't think the worst of people without proof. It was unlikely Fish would order a hit on his own flesh and blood; that specific kind of evil I associated with another party I'd known well enough to knock wood whenever her name came up. On the other hand, I wouldn't shake his hand if he offered it while I was hanging from a cliff. It would probably be one of those joke mitts you hold by a handle and then let go.

The score came up on-screen. It didn't look good for the favorite. He scowled, clawed a remote from a slash pocket, and switched off the monitor. He let the racquet fall to the mat at his feet and scooped a white terry towel off the handlebars of a stationary bike in a corner.

"Frank Wiener?" He used a corner of the towel to wipe his glasses, then mopped his face and the back of his neck. Most men who wear glasses look naked and weak when they take them off, but not this one. His eyes were fierce cobalt, custom-built for cross-examining defendants. "I imagine you get your share of ribbing with a name like that."

"I would, if it was mine."

He stopped mopping. The glasses were back on, but I felt the lasers just the same. For the second time on the same job I decided to turn up my cards. I was either a bad poker player or good enough to know when the other fellow had the hand I needed.

THIRTEEN

I snapped a cigarette out of the pack and lit it. "You're a politician," I said, "or you were. Maybe your license expired, but all the old skills wouldn't. You remember me, I think."

He lifted and resettled the spectacles, made wrinkles in the polished patches at the corners of his eyes. The sun came up behind a layer of smog. "An Old Testament name. Amos. A proletariat surname. Cooper? Wheeler?" He snapped his fingers, a sonic boom. "Walker. The Broderick case."

I had the cigarette between my fingers. I put it back between my lips and clapped my hands three times. "For a minute there I thought they'd nicked your brain when they pulled your face back under your collar. I wasn't sure if you'd see me. We didn't part on the best of terms."

He uncased two rows of teeth like polished headstones. "I can't say I remember the circumstances, but I make it a practice never to hold a grudge. People who have met me on the way up recognize me on the way down, and I might need them when the situation reverses again. As it does;

otherwise I wouldn't be in a position to make an appointment with anyone."

I bought that he didn't remember the circumstances the way I bought the Ambassador Bridge. But if he was willing to let it drift, I wasn't going to snag it back. "You know by now your beef with Velocity Financing just got cut in half," I said.

"If you're referring to Carl Fannon's death, I do. Now that I'm no longer in public office I can afford not to express regret I don't feel. A Quisling's a Quisling, alive or dead."

"What about Emil Haas?"

"It takes two to make a conspiracy. What's your interest in this?"

"I'm in it three ways. Yesterday morning, Fannon hired me to find Haas. He disappeared, he said. Then Haas came along and hired me to meet him in the basement of the Sentinel Building last night. The ink on that one wasn't dry when Haas's daughter Gwendolyn showed up and asked me the same thing Fannon asked. Three clients in one case is a personal best."

He made a wringing motion on the towel with both hands. "Wouldn't that fall under conflict of interest?"

"It would if I were working for one of them not to do what the others had hired me for. I'm not sure what you'd call making the same deal with the first and third and taking a little money on deposit to hear what the second had to say."

"Aren't you? I'd say unethical would cover it."

"No, just unusual. I didn't take any money from Gwendolyn and if I don't like what Haas wants of me I'll give him back his twenty. In order to do that I have to find him first. Which is what the others want." I took the cigarette out of my mouth, looked at it, and stuck it back in the pack. "I seem to be in some kind of conversational cloverleaf, talking my way right back around to where I started. I'm here to find out why Carl Fannon had a message from his office to call you. You didn't seem so chummy while you were accusing him of fronting for foreigners."

"That's not what you told my assistant. You said you had specific information on that very point."

"I also said my name was Frank Wiener. I didn't make all that up, by the way, just the Wiener part. I gave the real Frank some money last night to buy a package of wieners. He may have seen who locked Fannon in that vault, either on his way into the building or on his way out. Maybe both. The cops don't know that. I didn't think about it until I was halfway through the interview and then I didn't say it."

He twisted the towel tighter. "You met a man named Frank and bought him frankfurters."

"Yeah. Screwy enough to be true, isn't it? With a possible eyewitness in your pocket, and your resources, you could score big with the authorities. They might even reinstate you to the Bar."

"Why would I want that? I've got a job."

The room had only one window. A car whisked past on the street without making any noise. The walls were soundproof and the window was triple-glazed at least.

"Maybe you forgot our beef, but you remember me. I remember you. You don't care a fart in a whirlwind if Fannon and Haas sell Hart Plaza, Campus Martius, and the Detroit Lions to Russia and stick up a statue of Lenin in Grand Circus Park. You're looking to get back into the game. Maybe this time the mayor of Detroit or governor of the state. But before you swing that, you've got to erase the blot from your record. That costs plenty, and Fannon had plenty to spare. What did you dig up on him that'd be worth the grease you needed to lay off him?" I told him about the message on Fannon's wrist.

"So on top of nursing a hero complex I'm a blackmailer. What's to stop me from finding this Frank person myself? I have the resources, as you said."

"You don't know what he looks like, or if Frank is his name. You could comb the neighborhood for a month, and all you'd get is the runaround, even if you pay for the information. They might not know who you're asking about. That refrigerator-box crowd isn't as close as in the days of the hobo jungle. Or he might be a drifter already on his way to Denver in the back of a furniture van. Without a good physical description, you've got as much chance of finding him and breaking this case as you have of beating a real tennis player on a real court."

He slung the towel around his neck and hung on to both ends. "So why aren't you looking for him right now and breaking the case yourself? As I recall, you could stand to make a few brownie points with the authorities yourself."

"I stand to make more by keeping my nose out of an open investigation. All I'm interested in is doing what Fannon hired me for, finding Haas, and earning his twenty hearing what he has to say."

"I'd like to hear it myself." He stepped over to the window, and reached under the sill. Something clicked. In a little while the door opened and the pudgy feller came in, tucking his shirttail inside his pants. He was carrying his nifty portable phone.

FOURTEEN

The young feller's name was Richard, and it turned out he wasn't so young. He'd spent just enough time in medical college to find out he hadn't the stomach for it, three years' apprentice under a CPA until that party shipped out to Uruguay with a Cayman Island bank account number sewed inside his coat, dumb cluck that he was; Uruguay has an understanding with the U.S., and he'd spent most of what he'd chiseled fighting extradition. That was when Richard got the bright idea that his future lay in the law.

"Not that I plan to spend my life there," he'd said, while he was waiting for his phone to upload or whatever. "Most people in public office have an LLD."

Cecil Fish, who'd excused himself to shower after leaving specific instructions, came back on the end of this, pink as a tulip and wearing a taupe summer suit that looked as light as silk pajamas, moss-colored moccasins on his bare feet. He smelled of baby powder and the kind of cologne you put on with an eyedropper. "Most people in public office don't share their life stories with strangers."

"Yes, sir." The young man blushed to the ends of his fingers, then punched a key with one. "Here it is."

I held out my hand for it, but his boss snatched it from him, peered at it, then turned the screen my way.

"'Peaceable Shore,'" I read. "It sounds like the first line of a haiku. What's it mean?"

"If I knew that I wouldn't be sharing it. I'm hoping to make finding out part of our deal. You're something of a bloodhound, if I remember right. It came up on Velocity's e-mail correspondence, as a heading. They thought the account they used was impregnable, but even so it showed up just once and for less than thirty seconds before it vanished. I have to think it was read immediately and just as immediately deleted. In any case it was worth a fishing expedition—not to put the squeeze on him, but to see by his reaction if it was worth more digging on my part."

"How'd you get past Velocity's security?"

"My methods are my own. Rest assured they're legal. The Internet depends on the airwaves, and the FCC says those belong to the public. Some judges aren't so sure; but then when an independent moviemaker copied *The Great Train Robbery* scene-for-scene in 1903, the judge who heard the case ruled that since the original film wasn't physically stolen, there was no theft involved. The medium was new. So's the World Wide Web. I expect to be in my grave many years before it's ironed out. But I'm not dead yet."

"Okay, you hacked it. I'm not on the grid, so I should

care. I'm not convinced two words that don't mean anything to any of us is worth what I offered in return."

"I don't know that what you offered is worth what I just gave you." He uncovered the headstones. "We're just two farmers trading pigs in a poke, aren't we?"

"Why don't I spend a day or so on it, then if it goes ding get back to you?"

"What do *you* think, Richard?"

"What do you want me to think, Mr. Fish?"

He looked back at me. "You see, Richard agrees with me. Out with it, Walker; or I call the locals and charge you with blackmail. You came here under a fictitious name, intending to shake me down for some fuzzy connection to Carl Fannon's murder. It so happens I spent last night on Mackinac Island, attending a political convention. I'm sure you heard of it. It was on every station."

"Make it stick," I said.

"I can't. But until whoever you fall back on in these situations habeases you out; well, you know Iroquois Heights." He leaned forward and placed his hands tightly over Richard's ears. The assistant's face assumed a torturous grin, as if he'd gone through it all before. "You've pissed blood in the past, I'm sure," Fish whispered. "But none of us is getting any younger. Our kidneys don't bounce back like tennis balls anymore."

I grinned. I like my kidneys as well as anyone, but I'd already decided to tell him what he wanted. I just wanted to see if he was as miserable a son of a bitch as he used to be, and that was worth seeing the performance. I didn't buy that he'd found out about Peaceable Shore from the Internet. Postmodern technology spreads its legs for anyone, and it's just too easy to blame every little spill on that. I didn't buy it, but I was willing to rent it for the moment. Put two innocuous words together and they bent back the other direction. Put those two particular words together and they rang a note that I hadn't heard for so long I'd almost forgotten it; but it hurt an eardrum as if someone had tapped the mastoid with a tuning fork.

Couldn't be. I put the thought so far out of my head I felt like you do when you forget something important and your brain goes pleasantly blank, as if the thing had never been an issue. The human brain is like that, wiping out something too horrible for your emotions to accept: Freud's vacuum cleaner.

I made a show of getting out my notebook, but I hadn't recorded anything in it about Frank the wiener man; I hadn't thought him worth the trouble at the time. I described him from memory.

Richard looked up from the keyboard he was typing on. "Who's Edmund Fitzgerald?"

"I'll buy you the Gordon Lightfoot album," Fish said. "You're sure the tattoo was permanent?"

"A man who lives on ground-up hog snouts doesn't spend a lot of time soaking and peeling decals."

The young man was still pecking away. He seemed to be taking down the entire conversation. "I can print up flyers, distribute them among the interns. They can pass them around the homeless, offer what, fifty dollars if one turns him up?"

"Ten's plenty. They sleep with one eye open just to make sure they don't wake up naked. No sense keeping them awake around the clock." He looked at his watch. "Hightail it down to Frank Murphy Hall before it lets out for lunch. Take my car. Don't strip the gears. Ask for Roger Hurst. He sketches most of the trials where they don't let in cameras. Give *him* a hundred to break any appointments he's got this afternoon. Some of those bums can't read or don't know English. Don't come back without him."

Richard frowned at "bums," but got it all down.

Fish looked at me. "You don't mind hanging around to see he captures your man on paper."

"One hour in the Heights is already more than enough."

That was another thing I remembered about him, the color his face turned when the world didn't turn properly to suit him. Liverish, it used to be called, and it was an apt description. Now it's something else, probably no longer congestion; which is a word I associated with what happens in the outbound lanes when the whistle blows and everyone's in a hurry to get the hell out of Detroit, for which who can blame them? I'd been trying for forty years. But I'd dressed out my share of deer and stowed enough warm livers in the pouch I carried in my hunting coat to recognize that shade of purple.

Just short of the blowup I took a stiff folded sheet out of a pocket and snapped it open. The charcoal sketch was faithful to Frank, right down to the shipwreck on his chest. "The son of an old client majors in Art at Wayne State. I stopped by his dorm on the way."

I got away from there a little after three-thirty. The sheriff's car I'd seen earlier or one like it picked me up on the main stem and followed me long enough to run the plate, then boated down a side street; I'd hit a pothole full of mud a couple of days ago, hadn't stopped for a wash, and my car wasn't made in the right decade for the local dress code, but I didn't have any unpaid tickets or warrants outstanding and the deputy's shift was almost over. For a block and a half there I'd worn my shoulders up around my ears. But for once I crossed the city limits without leaving any brain cells behind. Things were looking up.

I didn't know if Peaceable Shore meant anything. I hoped it didn't mean what it might. At the very least I'd fobbed off investigating a homicide on someone who actually enjoyed chronic heartburn. At the very, *very* least I'd done the wiener man a good turn. He'd probably work a deal to swap out for whatever story he had to tell, spend a couple of hours in an air-conditioned room, maybe get a meal and a drink and a change of socks and underwear and enough cash to upgrade to Oscar Mayer for a week.

That's if he hadn't spun me and when he took up a big enough collection he'd upgrade to high-grade heroin instead. That thought put a cloud across my rosy dawn.

FIFTEEN

I stopped back at the office just long enough to call Barry Stackpole. He was as high-tech as they came, but refused to discuss anything confidential over a cell: Walmart scanners pick up those conversations all the time. It was another example of the applied paranoia that had kept him alive all these years. At its height, he'd carried his toothbrush to new quarters once every few days.

After five rings the recording kicked in offering to repeat-dial when my party was available. I hung up. Another thing Barry never did was use an answering machine.

The bottom had fallen out of the city, dumping traffic in all directions. I crawled along with it and pulled into my garage just shy of five, ran some water into a glass in the kitchen and filled it the rest of the way from the bottle I kept in the cabinet above the sink. Municipal water direct from the tap is a hell of a thing to do to good liquor, but I was out of ice and feeling too frail to drink it straight.

In the living room sitting in the only comfortable chair in the house I watched the news. A container ship and an

Asian airliner were missing, the Middle East had taken another step back into the eleventh century, a priest was under indictment for building a thirty-room mansion from the poor fund, a movie star had come out of the closet, and a pitchers' duel between the Tigers and the Blue Jays was threatening to bleed into football season. The rerun channel was playing a loud sitcom from the seventies. The rest was all zombies, all the time. I switched off the set and picked up the phone. This time Barry answered.

"Peaceable Shore," he said. "Sounds like a cult. Nothing else?"

"You know how it is. Some days the leads come in gushers, others like cheese fermenting."

"It has a generic sound. Probably get a hundred hits."

"So would my source, which is why he palmed it off on me so easy. But he didn't have the association I have with it, so it might not have clicked with him."

"Who's the source?"

"Our old friend Cecil Fish."

"Oh, Christ. What's the association?"

I told him. He said Oh Christ again. "Impossible. I witnessed her execution through the pirate feed from North Korea, along with millions of others."

"Me, too, along with millions more, cleaned up on TV for the squeamish. But these days you can't trust your eyes. They can fake the Ayatollah scarfing down the blue plate special at Bob Evans and fool all his wives."

"Forensics experts were sent from every country that issued warrants. They came back satisfied."

"I wasn't invited."

"DNA samples checked."

"I heard."

"Couldn't be her," he said.

"Couldn't be her," I said.

"Jesus, do you think it's her?"

"Can you deliver or not?"

"Have I ever let you down?"

"Yeah."

"Just what the hell are you working on, Amos?"

"I'm sitting on that for now."

"Thanks for the vote of confidence, you son of a bitch."
He said he'd call back and the conversation ended.

I cradled the receiver, grinning. You can trust some people with money, others with your girl, and maybe one or two with your life; you can rarely trust any one of them with all those things, but I trusted Barry with them. But when it came to information, he'd pry open the poor box to buy it. I'd known him as a war correspondent, a newspaper columnist, a cable TV reporter, a web master, a blogger, and all the other things connected with spreading news through the process of modern evolution. He was absolutely fearless— three sticks of dynamite and a menu of missing parts had proven that—and I'd depend on him to defend me against any threat; but until I got a handle on the current client's business I didn't trust him with a crumb he could feed the big gaping maw of public curiosity.

Not even me, who'd given him blood during the nine hours the surgeons at Detroit Receiving spent reassembling him.

I was turning off the lights when the phone rang. It wasn't as bad as predicted, Barry said. Out of sixty-odd hits, all but eleven eliminated themselves on the face of the nature of their activities; one, a charitable foundation, listed the UN Secretary-General on its board of directors. Three of those were based in European countries on good terms with the U.S. and seemed safe to table. Four were scattered between five hundred and a thousand miles from Detroit; those I could put off until the rest bombed out, forcing me to split my fee with other agencies. Four were local. All showed promise. I thanked Barry, assured him he'd be the first in his field to know if there was anything juicy, and set my alarm for six A.M., early enough to fix an old-fashioned farm breakfast. There was no telling when I'd eat next.

SIXTEEN

The Cutlass started with a grunt of surprise; its motor hadn't turned over at that hour of the morning in years. Yawning, I gave the steering wheel a sympathetic pat and pulled out of the garage onto asphalt pocked with holes and dark with dew. Drops sparkled on the grass. It would be an hour or more before it dried enough to wake up the sprinklers. Traffic was light in town, made up mostly of American-made cars driven by the red-eye shift at Ford, General Motors, and Chrysler with their lamps on.

The first place on my list—because it was the farthest and the day was fresh—was in Warren, a stone's throw from the GM Tech Center. That was a going concern around the clock. Test drivers shoved their shiny new plastic toys at top speed around the track and the city-size parking lot was packed fender-to-fender while the eggheads were climbing into their lab coats inside the huge dome-shaped research building.

I passed a mile or so of chain link fence and left the pavement for a stretch of gravel bisecting what had obviously been a large dairy farm. The large whitewashed two-story farmhouse had a new metal roof and two silos flanked a barn the size and shape of an airplane hangar. A sign on a concrete slab showed a stylized sailboat floating on a wiggly blue line toward a mound with a palm tree sticking up from it. Under the picture:

PEACEABLE SHORE

A Haven for the Renewed

Twenty-some people were hoeing rows of green plants in an acre of plowed ground, with two more manhandling panels of galvanized iron on the roof of the barn. The web site Barry had found advertised the place as a recovery center of some kind.

A gravel turnaround looped in front of a long front porch supporting a row of unoccupied bentwood rockers and a butter churn with geraniums sprouting from the top. Someone had taped a square of cardboard over the doorbell, asking visitors in block Sharpie letters to knock. Pigtails of red, yellow, and green wires spilled beyond the sign's edges ending in wire nuts. I rapped on a screen door, releasing tiny helicopters of peeled paint from the wooden frame and a sifting of rust from the iron mesh. Darkness behind, broken up by geometric patterns of sunlight spilling in through windows on the other side of the house.

A distant door opened, releasing just enough illumination to describe the boundaries of a long narrow hall dividing the ground floor into two halves. The rectangle of light framed a substantial body in a bell-shaped dress. Another door with a glass insert opened halfway along the hall, letting in more light and the same body, larger now in appearance. By the time it reached the screen door, it seemed to fill the passage from wall to wall. A bare arm the size of a leg of lamb reached up, tinkled a hook loose, pushed open the door against the grinding complaint of a spring, and I was face-to-face with the largest woman I'd ever seen. She balanced three hundred pounds on a six-foot-four-inch frame, with another hundred pounds of strawberry-blond hair falling to her waist on both sides of her print blouse. Her face was an assembly of ovals bunched around a pug nose and a tiny mouth painted fireplug red. Patches of rouge stained the ovals of her cheeks and her eyes glistened like pennies in a wishing well. A gust of the kind of perfume they stirred up in steel drums came out with the suction of the door opening.

She said nothing, waiting.

I fished out a card and held it level with the pennies. "We're conducting a missing-person investigation, and the name Peaceable Shore came up. I'd like to ask you a couple of questions."

The other leg of lamb rose and a stunted-looking hand took the card. That hand was a disappointment, sprouting like a child's pinwheel at the end of that arm. At that it was twice the size of mine. The tiny lips writhed over the printed words. "Who's 'we'?" The pennies wandered past my shoulder to the empty Cutlass.

I smiled. "We's me. The plural sounds more official. Actually I've got all the authority of a Cub Scout. I'd consider it a personal favor if you could spare me a few minutes so I can move on from here."

Her neck accordioned while she consulted a tiny octagonal gold watch sunk into the suet of her wrist like a micro-chip. "Five minutes. I've got a referral on the way and one stranger's enough in their condition." She stepped aside, still holding the screen door.

The place smelled like Grandma's, cheap furniture oil mixed with apple-nut bread baking somewhere. Behind me she closed and rehooked the door and I flattened against the wall to let her take the lead. I followed her between shoulder-high wainscoting, watching her tea-colored muslin skirt swing from side to side like a bell without a clapper, a pair of muscular calves ending in black walking shoes, no ankles in between, the floor planks shifting under her weight. Her hair in back also reached her waist, or where a waist be-longed. I figured her for a retired Olympics shot-putter, if not a transsexual slaughterhouse employee.

I put all that aside when we passed through a door marked PRIVATE at the end of the hall and she sidled around a gray steel desk with a composition top and sat with her back to a framed diploma on the wall. Someone named Lois Cham-pion had graduated from a Neuropathy program in Min-neapolis with a degree in mental and physical therapy.

"*Dr.* Champion?" I asked, sitting in a vinyl-upholstered kitchen chair opposite her.

"Mrs." She settled into the space between the arms of her chair; I thought of a bear relapsing into its rings of tallow. She picked up my card from the desk where she'd put it, without looking at it this time. "I doubt I can help you, Mr. Walker. All our people are present and accounted for. We take the roll in the morning and do a bed check at night."

"Rehab?"

"No. They come here from drug and alcohol rehabilitation clinics to prepare for returning to the outside world."

"Halfway house?"

The ovals bunched in displeasure; I thought. Considering the amount of spatial and weight displacement, she might have been stroking out or suppressing a burp. "I never use the term. We had difficulty obtaining a permit to use this property because the neighbors thought they'd be living next door to ex-convicts. Many of our guests have violated no laws except those that apply to controlled substances. The more severe cases stole from relatives to support their habit."

"I don't get it. Rehab places are supposed to prepare them to return to society. How many hoops do they have to jump through before they can apply for a driver's license?"

"You don't know the statistics. Alcohol and drug abuse is the twenty-first-century's answer to the Black Plague. The clinics have their hands full detoxing the residents, and only so many beds to restrain them during the process. They can't spare any to piece together their shattered souls once they've gotten the poison out of their system. Without places like Peaceable Shore, their chances of remaining straight are next to nothing."

"Okay." I changed positions on the uncomfortable seat. I wanted to smoke, but I supposed she'd consider that abuse of a controlled substance. "Why do you think the name of your establishment came up while I was looking for Emil Haas?"

The ovals shifted again. "I know that name."

"He and his partner are investors. They've been buying up delinquent properties in Detroit for renting and resale.

The partner hired me to find Haas after he vanished. Carl Fannon's the partner's name." I watched her, but all that flesh was an almost impenetrable insulation between me and what was going on behind it.

She returned my card to the desk, squaring the corners in its exact center.

"The murder, yes; if that's what it was. I was right, I'm no help. I know nothing more of either man than what I've heard and seen on the news. The only offers I've received on this property are from an auto dealership looking to expand and a developer who wants to glut what little is left of open country with McMansions, basketball hoops, and speed bumps. I turned them down—despite the profit I would make. I didn't spend four years studying the bundle of nerves that is the human corpus in order to drink Cosmopolitans in Myrtle Beach."

"You're the owner?"

She flattened her palms on top of her desk, her face reddening until it blended with the blush on her cheeks, and rose. "That's as much time as I can give you, Mr. Walker. I'm sorry."

"No need. You'd be surprised how many places call themselves Peaceable Shore. This one's just another bead on the abacus. Mind if I look around outside, just so I can say I did?"

"I thought your client was dead."

"He was. Still is, I suppose, but his check cleared before he died."

"I can't honor your request. I was serious about how many strange faces my guests can tolerate at this point in their passage. I'm not running a petting zoo. I employ people to maintain the safety of the people I'm responsible for." She peeled the card off her desk and held it out.

"That's all right, Mrs. Champion. I found out it costs just as much to print five hundred as to print one, and they wear out so fast, the way people keep picking them up and laying them down."

I used the succession of doors. It was like passing through the various chambers leading from a plant room. As I put distance between us I felt the pressure relieving, like the change of temperatures from one climate-controlled enclosure to another, but I hadn't heard the door to her office close and was sure she was watching me in case I doubled back or ducked down one of the halls to right and left. When the screen clapped shut behind me I breathed in the smells of cut grass and sunshine, but I knew I'd be smelling baked apples and lemon Pledge the rest of the day.

SEVENTEEN

The watching went on, if only in my head, as I swung the car around and drove back to the road. A paved intersection at the end of a country block changed to limestone a few hundred yards after I turned onto it and I towed a plume of white dust for a quarter-mile, where a gravel road crossed my path, slicing the rural section into a perfect square of mostly turned earth: From the air, that part of Wayne County would look like a brownie pan. Now I was looking at the farmhouse's sagging back porch and the other side of the barn from a distance of some sixty acres. The gardening guests were still at work, but other figures in what might have been green work clothes but were probably uniforms wandered about, apparently aimlessly. That would be the security patrol. They weren't carrying rifles or shotguns, and I was too far away to see if they wore handguns. I didn't have to. People have a certain way of walking when they're packing pistols on their hips.

Nature and prudence had provided windbreaks in the form of mounds of unworked dirt anchored by weeds and rocks heaved up by a restless planet. It looked like Lyme-tick country, so after I got out of the car and tossed my coat and tie into the backseat I tucked my pants cuffs into the tops of my socks. It made me look like Little Boy Blue and wouldn't do a damn bit of good against a determined arach-nid, but no one likes to admit he's helpless against assault. That's why they make fallout shelters.

Ten feet in I spooked a garter snake sunning itself on a patch of clay, and when I came down from the stratosphere I picked up a fallen walnut branch about two feet long to swat at its more venomous relatives. We only have one of those in Michigan, and massasauga rattlers rate down around bumblebees. Sue me. I'm a city boy and prefer my enemies with legs.

As the sun climbed I began to perspire. Although it wasn't as hot as it would be later in the season, the ground was un-even and I worked up a sweat stumbling over hard clods of dirt and straddling molehills. I was limping now, thanks to an old encounter with a high-powered rifle in similar coun-try. If I tripped or turned an ankle stepping into soft earth and broke something, it would be just my luck that one of Mrs. Champion's human pit bulls would be the first to find me. We were minutes away from one of the busiest cities in the state, but I had the impression Peaceable Shore consid-ered itself an island outside all other jurisdictions.

Halfway across, I got someone's attention. One of the uniformed security guards turned his face my direction, climbed into a frog-green two-seater ATV, and charged. He kept the little motor wound up tight, bucking over the ruts and nearly separating himself from the automatic rifle slung over his right shoulder. That was careless bordering on criminal. I had his measure then: The weapon was just part of his costume, all straps and buckles and boots to his knees.

Which made him twice as dangerous as a professional. You never know what an amateur will do next, even more than he does. I reached behind my hip bone and touched the Chief's Special to make sure it was still riding in its holster.

He throttled down a few yards shy of where I stood, shut the ignition, sprang out, and swung the automatic rifle free of his shoulder; all the motions straight from the Gospel According to Jason Bourne. I spread my own feet with hands out from my hips, trying not to seem like I'd done the same thing a thousand times out of a thousand.

"This is private property, mister," he said. "Maybe you missed the signs." You could slice cheese with his Kentucky twang.

There hadn't been any signs, but I didn't argue the point. "Sorry, brother," I said. "I'm scouting out property; thought I might get to know the neighborhood."

He relaxed a little then; at least the rifle drooped a little from its strap. "I wouldn't know. Personally, I'm saving up for a condo on Jefferson. Let the darkies cut the grass and pop a cold one watching the rich folks sail up and down the De-troit River."

"Give us the money, we'll show 'em how to be rich."

"Ain't that the truth." He pointed the barrel of the rifle toward the road. "Don't come back this way."

Just then the wind gusted up from behind him, lifting a flap of blue tarpaulin covering a heap in the box behind his seat. I smelled unprocessed marijuana. Just for fun I drew the green aroma in sharply through my nostrils, held it, and let it out, grinning. He answered with a grimace. I turned around and tramped back to my car.

A rehab unit that furnished drugs to its residents could stay in business longer than Coca-Cola; but that brought me no closer to who had killed Carl Fannon—and where I could find Emil Haas—than I'd been at the start.

The next ball in the pocket was closer to home. It was a former warehouse on East Atwater, close enough to the water to spritz yourself with Detroit River when the wind blew from Windsor. It had stored bags of seed, iron felloes, and stove parts when Taft waddled around the White House, moved crates of Canadian whisky on greased rails under Volstead, and sheltered hundreds of ragged drifters at New Deal time before a new set of squatters stank it up with reefers and patchouli. A syndicate of doctors in Bloomfield Hills had rescued it from demolition, converted it to condos for silicone-chip sultans, but then the century had turned with a ponderous rumble and squashed their portfolios flat. Now the new half-million-dollar roof covered a Goodwill drop-off, a movie soundstage empty since Hollywood emigrated back West, a padlocked meth lab, and the next Peaceable Shore on my list.

The doorbell summoned a human pipe ladder draped in a faded green caftan that ended in a pool around his feet. His cowl cast his face entirely in shadow. I gave him the friendly stranger's grin.

"Scythe out being sharpened?"

"I get that a lot. I'm Rector North." His voice belonged to a man three times his bulk, deep and resonant.

"I'm Brother Walker." I held up one of my cards. A pair of eye-whites flickered deep inside the cowl, reading without raising a hand to accept it. The wide sleeves of his robe covered both almost to the fingertips.

"We're forbidden to touch anything from outside."

"Moral contagion?"

"Physical. Infection can be fatal."

"I've had my distemper shot." But I put the card away. "I'm investigating a death for a client. Did you know a man named Carl Fannon?"

"The name isn't familiar. I'm assuming he's the man afflicted with death."

"That's a nice way of putting it. The not-so-nice one is he was murdered. May I ask what you do here?"

"Everything except sweep the floors. Such work is therapeutic for the residents."

"Would you mind?" I swept both hands back from my neck. "I feel like I'm talking to the Dutch Maid."

He hesitated, then raised his arms and pushed back the cowl. He was younger than he sounded, but he was as bald as a peeled egg and his face was patched with running lesions. He looked like a topographical map that hadn't set properly. A pair of cloudless blue eyes mocked my reaction. "Psoriasis. Not leprosy. This is a dermatological clinic. I'm a nurse. As you can see, I'm empathetic."

"Why Rector?"

"Rector's my given name." A set of perfect teeth flashed in the ravaged face. "Did you think this was some kind of cult?"

"The thought crossed my mind. I've missed a couple of medical journals," I said. "When did you go from scrubs to Harry Potter?"

He smoothed the front of the caftan with his hands, which turned out to be encased in flesh-colored latex gloves. "Insulation. It's required from heat as well as cold. Some of us are like skinned rabbits. Would you like to have a look?"

"I'm in the information business. It never hurts to stock up."

The space had been partitioned off from the rest of the building, but it was an open plan. People in various stages of dress—a few might have been naked—sat at tables or on chairs and sofas, reading, knitting, building model ships and planes, scrolling cell phone screens, watching TV, or staring off into space. A girl of about eighteen sat combing her fingers through a fall of glistening black hair veiling her features completely; her bare shoulders in a tank top were peeling like old paint.

White smears of cream, possibly zinc-based, turned some of the faces into masks. Others, uncovered, resembled underdone pastry. Bits of translucent flakes stirred in the ambient air on every horizontal surface, glistening like fish scales on a wharf. They'd be spending most of their time sloughing.

"It's not as bad as it looks," said Rector North in low tones. "Not all of it, anyway. Many of our residents hold full-time jobs, depending on the tolerance of employers and their colleagues. All are being treated free of charge by some of the top specialists in the world. They come here to learn everything they can about the disease. I don't know the man you mentioned, Mr. Walker. My acquaintances are limited to fellow sufferers."

"What about Emil Haas? He was Fannon's partner before he went missing."

He shook his head carefully, as if to avoid throwing a piece of his flesh into my eye. "Both names are vaguely familiar."

"They're investment barons, lately involved in buying up urban real estate. The name Peaceable Shore came up during my investigation. You should trademark the name. You've got competitors operating under the same handle."

"Not precisely competitors. This is the only residential clinic specializing in psoriasis in the continental United States."

"Is it a painful condition?"

"You mean beyond the stigma? It can be excruciating."

I looked around one last time, then took out my notebook, turned it to the page with the address of the Peaceable Shore in Warren, and showed it to him. "Talk to Mrs. Champion. She may be able to arrange a connection."

I ran aground on the Peaceable Shore in Romulus. Black letters snapped into a white panel set perpendicular to Vining Road read:

> P   CEA L   S ORE
> WELCO E   O   D TRO T

The fact that it belonged to a place that advertised itself as a spa didn't predispose me to be welcomed to Detroit by something called "Piecemeal Sore." The small, flat-roofed building was identical to the galvanized-iron offices of the chain of privately owned parking lots that lined the road, and had probably been used by a competitor before it was squeezed out of business and its acreage crowded to a narrow apron around the structure. Its driveway ended at the road; but for that and a half-mile of chain link and razor wire on the other side, it would have extended directly into a runway belonging to Detroit Metropolitan Airport. As I stepped out onto the crumbling asphalt, a sleek red-tailed propeller jet with the FedEx logo painted on its fuselage chirped to a landing, roared up to within yards of the fence, and swung ninety degrees toward the terminals at the far end. I unclenched my buttocks and mounted the concrete slab that served as the front porch.

The usual cluster of decals advertising the Moose, Elks, Masons, and the rest of the brotherhoods decorated a green-painted steel slab without a handle or a knob: I would have to be buzzed inside. I pointed a finger at the hard-rubber button mounted next to the frame, then read a printed notice taped to the door, announcing that the establishment had been closed by order of the sheriff's office. I figured the sign had hung there since just before the county elections. That's when the authorities usually notice that the massage parlors operating in their jurisdiction offer more than shiatsu. Most of the personnel are Korean nationals and can't vote.

I looked at my watch. It was coming up on two o'clock, and the last place on my list was clear out in Ypsilanti by the Rawsonville Ford plant. My sausages and fried potatoes were wearing off. I ate a sandwich and drank a beer in a tavern in downtown Romulus and drove to Barry Stackpole's place. I wanted to ask him if he could dig up anything more on the Peaceable Shore in Warren. I was beginning to like that place, and not just because the smell of marijuana made me nostalgic for my youth.

He was living in a house in the old Corktown district, on the cusp between the vanishing Irish and the burgeoning Mexican population, close enough to Most Holy Trinity Church to feel the chill when its Norman spires cast it in shadow. The fact that he'd signed a two-year lease was evidence he was settling down; either that, or he'd just gotten tired of the Bedouin life. He still had a prosthetic leg and a patch on his skull to remind him of why he'd become a moving target in the first place, but since the people who make bombs have broadened their objective to include private citizens along with muckraking journalists, he was just as unsafe traveling as standing still.

It was a turn-of-the-twentieth-century bungalow that would smell of corned beef and cabbage every time a resident broke through the plaster. The present owner had painted it a cheerful yellow, trimmed it with white, and replaced all the original wood-sash windows with double-glazed panes in aluminum frames; a homey little place that went with Barry's personality like Raggedy Ann with G.I. Joe.

But his less paranoid circumstances didn't make me feel any more secure when I saw his front door was ajar. Nobody does that in Detroit.

At least, nobody who owns the door.

EIGHTEEN

I didn't touch the door or call out his name. I went back to the car, retrieved the .38 I'd transferred to the glove compartment in order to drive comfortably, checked the cylinder, and recrossed the sidewalk, holding the gun down alongside my leg to avoid drawing attention from the neighbors. A trigger-happy town had gotten worse since concealed-carry went viral.

I palmed the door open slowly in case the hinges needed oiling, flattening my back against it and pivoting inside with it. The house was a square box, no deeper than it was wide, with the living room taking up most of the space. Barry had torn out a partition from between it and the kitchen, allowing sunlight to stream in from the eastern side. It made the place even more cheerful and deepened the sense of dread. Sections of the *Free Press* made tents on the rug, and there was a sticky-looking ceramic mug and a scrap of toast on a saucer on the coffee table; bachelor stuff. No signs that anyone had put up a fight.

An open arch led into the small dining room, which Barry

had turned into his office. He never turned off his computer. The flat-screen monitor on the retired FBI shooting stand he used for a desk made little gasping noises shifting screen-saver images: mug shots of mostly dead mobsters, a pair of shiny shoes poking out the end of a striped sheet some sensitive cop had spread over a corpse on a barbershop floor, a courtroom shot of a *capo* currently residing in the federal corrections house in Milan, Michigan, towing his oxygen tank; all Barry's stock-in-trade. The cooling fan whirred in the tower. His swivel chair with its built-in orthopedic support stood slightly off-center, waiting for a reunion with his sore back. A Maker's Mark bottle stood three-quarters-full where his right elbow belonged, next to a squat thick-bottomed glass. I sniffed at the glass, twisted the cap off the bottle, sniffed at that, and swallowed a bracer straight from the neck. I don't like bourbon as a rule, but this was a me-dicinal situation.

I doubted his computer would enlighten me even if I knew how to work the thing. He'd told me more than once he'd rigged all his devices to play dumb whenever he went offline, and his firewall was better than Langley's.

The door opposite the desk was open a few inches. I pushed it the rest of the way with the barrel of the gun and looked at an unmade bed, a copy of *Hour Detroit* lying open facedown on a nightstand, some clothes in a closet, more clothes in a three-drawer bureau. I pushed around the shirts in the top drawer, picked up a Glock Fifty, sprang out the magazine, put the muzzle to my nose. It was loaded up tight, with one in the chamber, and hadn't been fired since its last cleaning.

I knew then Barry hadn't left on his own. He might have

grown complacent enough to venture out unarmed, but he wouldn't leave the weapon at home without locking his door.

Back in the living room I checked his answering machine. The robo-voice that came with the instrument told me there were no messages. I tried redial. An operator answered. I hung up without saying anything. Barry automatically dialed O every time he finished a conversation. Star sixty-nine was just as unhelpful; he'd fixed a way to keep anyone from finding out who'd called him most recently.

No, his enemies couldn't trace him. But neither could his friends. This one was left to wonder if he'd gotten himself in trouble or if I'd brought it to him.

Lieutenant Child worked out of 1300 Beaubien, still the Detroit Police Department's official headquarters until more space opened up in the old third precinct where most of the staff had emigrated. The original, from the outside an impressive Deco pile overlooking the lively Greektown neighborhood, was rotting from the top down, kind of like the city, and most of the personnel had moved to the lower floors to lessen the impact when the collapse began. It smelled of dry rot and pre-war cigars.

The situation was just as cramped, so he'd forfeited the privacy of his own office for a steel desk in a corner by a window with a view of the Greektown Casino, where the owners had erected a scaffold to redo the façade along the lines of the out-of-state chain that had bought it. Either he was a masochist or he chose the site to remind himself to stay on his toes. A few months earlier, an off-duty armored car guard had walked up to a cash truck parked in front of the casino, told the guard on duty to open the hatch, and walked away lugging half a million dollars in cash in sacks. That insult, committed right under the DPD's nose, had led to an arrest in record time. A run-of-the-mill homicide could wait while that one was processed.

In a suit without stripes he looked even wider top-side than before. Hair cuttings pasted the collar of this outfit, same as the last, but they hadn't been there more than a day. He must have liked his barber well enough to overlook his shortcomings with brush and blower, to visit him at least twice a week.

He heard me out, running a broad palm across his already showroom-smooth chin. The clock plugged into the wall behind him made sizzling noises in the silence after.

"Gone less than forty-eight, you say?" he asked then.

"I just talked to him yesterday. But if you knew his history you'd know he didn't leave on his own, so let's wave that rubbish about protocol."

IIe wasn't the arguing type. He lifted his receiver, made the report, and hung up. "Deb Stonesmith's running Missing Persons now. She don't let the grass grow."

"She doesn't. I met her when she was with Major Crimes, before they broke it up. Thanks, Lieutenant."

"You think you hit a nerve at one of those Peaceable Shore places?"

"Barry's got his own set of enemies, but the timing's interesting. I didn't mention his name in either of them, but it wouldn't be hard to trace me to an old news story or two with his byline. It's no great leap from there to figuring out he's my main information broker. Seal him off and I'm half blind." I'd told him about the rehab place in Warren with its own drug-delivery service and the skin treatment center on the river. He stopped me when I got to the massage parlor by the airport.

"We cooperated with County on that one. It was one of a string owned by a South Korean national that got himself booted to Buddha when he tried to move in on a competitor. The feds shut down the others. He was too lawyered up for us to waste the taxpayers' time on him before; but things have a way of working themselves out, don't they?"

"Sometimes. Most times they need a nudge."

"Meaning from someone with big fat elbows like you."

"I didn't say that."

He spotted one of the loose clippings, pried it loose with a fingernail, studied it like an entomologist examining a bug, and scraped it off on the edge of his tin wastebasket. "Offhand, the skin joint's the place to start, given its history. Except you didn't make any contact there."

"If someone saw me, recognized me, made the connection to Barry, and moved at the speed of light to scoop him up. I don't buy it."

"Me either." He snapped open a handkerchief and wiped the barber slickum off his finger. "I'll see what the boys in Narc have on the Warren operation; that Atwater crowd too. I imagine the Mexican miracle drug's just as popular with them itch-scratchers. Could be your friend's been raking some muck in that racket. They saw your card, and like you say, you and Stackpole aren't a state secret.

"I'd like it better if this has something to do with our business downtown," he said then. "My money's still on Haas. I like things nice and obvious."

"Anything new there?"

"Nope. The daughter don't know anything. You?"

"You've got what I've got."

"Okay for now." He was looking at me the same way he'd looked at that rogue hair. "This isn't a blank check. You got two detectives bending the rules and flirting with the wrong end of influence-peddling, and cops can hold a grudge till it screams, especially when they think you're playing things too close to the buttons."

"I've heard that one, Lieutenant. I can sing it word-for-word in the shower."

"Brother, you never been so naked as you are right now."

I calculated the odds of spilling what I suspected against each minute I sat facing his desk, got up, and left, not forgetting to thank him for his time. Mom always said a kind word is a pass into heaven.

NINETEEN

When I got back to the hutch, Gwendolyn Haas was sitting on the padded bench in the room where customers trickled in to count the bubbles in the wallpaper, stroking the screen of a handheld device with a thumb. The palette today was slate-blue, from silk blouse to starched skirt to modest heels. It was an even better choice for her red hair and pale skin, and a woman with legs as good as hers should have done away with slacks entirely. It made up for the slight spread of her waist. Well, we were all taking up more space than fashion intended.

I couldn't tell if she'd been waiting five minutes or all day, and maybe neither could she. That three-by-five screen sucked people into a void where time had no value.

"Your magazines are stale," she said without looking up. "But then, who reads them anymore?"

For once I had no comeback. I unlocked the door to the confessional and stood aside. She got up, her stiff skirt rustling, and went in past me, still thumbing her doohickey.

Only when she was back in the customer's chair did she put it in her purse—a blue one this time, to match her outfit, slightly smaller than a golf bag—and look around. "You made a joke about a ficus, but you should have some kind of plant. It creates the illusion of life."

"Not when you forget to water it." I sat down, took a half-turn in the swivel, and broke a bottle of good Scotch out of the safe. It was a birthday present; I made a note to send myself a thank-you card. "Join me?" I selected two glasses from the stationery drawer and set them on the desk. "No ice, sorry. I can cut it from the tap, if you don't mind a little rust."

I made the offer half-expecting to offend her into leaving. I was feeling cranky. She called my bluff. "I can use the iron. I'm anemic."

In the little water closet I poured two inches, went back, and stained it a pale gold, watching her. She observed the operation without nodding until it turned the shade of old bronze. I brought my own glass to the same level, without water.

"Don't read anything into this," I said, twisting the cap back on. "I'm a little bruised today."

She picked up her glass, drank off the top, and sat back cradling it. Her skim-milk cheeks pinkened slightly. "Me, too. I heard from Dad."

I sliced off the same amount. "In person or over the phone?"

"Neither." She moved a bunch of junk around inside her bag, drew out a Number 10 envelope, and flipped it onto the desk. "Someone slid it under the door of my apartment, sometime this morning. I was up late last night. It was there when I got up."

I looked at it without picking it up. There was no writing on it, just the Velocity logo with the hollow *V* with racing lines running through it on cream-colored rag stock.

"I was careful to handle it by the edges." She shrugged when I looked at her blankly. "Fingerprints."

"Oh, no one bothers with those anymore. It's all genetics now." I drank again.

"Aren't you going to open it and read it?"

"Tell me what's in it."

"But it's right there!"

"You couldn't prove that by me. All I know is what you said; which is what I'll tell the cops if they ask. They have to ask. Hearsay isn't evidence. I can't go to jail for withholding it. If I were to read what you say is in that envelope, and it's what you say it is, I'd be required to report that you had direct contact with the chief suspect in Carl Fannon's murder; which is what your father is unless and until he comes forward and is exonerated. Then they wouldn't have to ask. Do you want the cops to know you heard from him?"

All trace of pink had vanished. "Dad and I have some issues, but what kind of daughter would I be if I gave him up and somehow he goes to prison for a crime he didn't commit?"

"A bitch."

The man who invented litmus paper got the idea from a redhead. Her face flushed so deep her freckles vanished. Her knuckles whitened gripping the bag, but she didn't smack me with it. "For someone who works for me, you seem to be giving all the orders."

"If you knew which ones to give, you wouldn't need me. Right now I'm wishing I'd taken money from you so I could make the grand gesture and give it back. Am I fired?"

I watched her mood ring of a face shift colors, hoping for red again so I'd be down to two clients, one dead, the other missing; the best kind when it came to having to drop everything and make a report.

"I don't like walking on eggs," she said.

"No one does, Miss Haas. Take it from someone who does it for a living."

She breathed in and out, admired the view through the window, nodded, looked back at me. "He said not to worry about him, that he's just gone somewhere to think and that I mustn't think he's in hiding for anything he's done, but rather to avoid doing something he finds distasteful. That's the word he used, 'distasteful.' It was always one of his favorites when he felt his partner was stepping over the line. Father looked upon himself as the conscience of the firm. He talked Carl out of some deals that would have put them on the cover of *Fortune*, just because they struck him as shady." She leaned forward and tapped the envelope. "I took it from this that this was one of those times when Carl refused to pull out."

I made a quarter-turn toward the window to see what had caught her eye. A river gull had lit on the roof of the pseudo-pub across the street and was nibbling lice from under one wing. People who'd swing a shovel at a rat throw peanuts to gulls and pigeons because they have feathers. "I'm glad you didn't tell me about this, Miss Haas."

"But I—Oh." She turned paler than when she'd come in. "You mean the police could use this as evidence he killed Carl Fannon."

"He had means and opportunity, and a dandy motive like smiting his partner in a noble cause could turn a grubby local prosecutor into a national celebrity. That empty bank vault in the Sentinel Building would go on display in the FBI museum next to O.J.'s glove."

"You won't tell anyone we had this conversation."

"We didn't."

She nodded again and picked up the envelope. The flap was open and a corner of the sheet folded inside stuck up a quarter-inch, jagged where someone had trimmed it with scissors, probably to remove a printed letterhead. It was dusty pink with a thin green stripe running up the edge.

I said, "Have you got any cash in that duffel?"

"Twenty or thirty dollars. Why?"

"Give me twenty. That makes you my client officially. When the cops bust me for accessory after the fact, I'll at least have something to tell them better than I'm working for a dead man."

"Does that mean you have something to go on?" The milk face curdled. "You held out on me until I could put something in your pocket?"

I said something not entirely under my breath. "Lady, if I was going to go to that kind of trouble, don't you think I'd have held you up for a C-note at least?"

After she left I picked up the crisp pair of tens she'd put on the desk. Alexander Hamilton looked even smugger than usual, with good reason. Not because I'd now squizzen forty dollars out of the Haases on the same investigation, but because my bad luck was holding. If I'd been looking in another direction, I'd have missed that pink-and-green stationery in Gwendolyn's envelope, sent by her father; all it would have taken was half a second. As long as I had a lead I was still on the case, and how I got it could put me in the tank down the hall from Emil Haas.

TWENTY

Barry still had connections high enough up in the *News* to get me into the morgue, where a woman in shoulder pads and a floppy bow tie typed my request into a computer and left me standing at the counter long enough to wonder if *Working Girl* had been the last movie she'd seen before going underground. The room took up all the square footage in the basement where in times past the great cylinder presses had set the building rocking on its foundation; gone to scrap, now. Fluorescents glowed through semi-opaque panels onto open steel shelves with aisles in between, supporting plat-size books of bound early numbers and more recent issues in bright yellow microfilm boxes and discs in plastic cases. Almond-colored file drawers lined a wall that went back into infinity like some gothic scene in a Coen Brothers film. They would contain prints and negatives of all the photos the newspaper had published since Teddy Roosevelt's last whistle-stop visit.

The space was shared, like the building itself, by the *News* and *Free Press*, formerly fierce competitors, but now grafted together by a Joint Operating Agreement intended to stave off the inevitable. They share advertising, confidential sources, and pączkis on Fat Tuesday. Most of their circulation eats supper at four o'clock and is in bed by nine. What will we use to wrap our fish and line our birdcages when the last newspaper turns out its lights?

Somewhere on the far edge of the universe a metal drawer rumbled open and banged shut a minute later. A couple of light years after that, the woman reappeared carrying a stack of gray cardboard folders and thumped them down on the counter. She handed me a clipboard.

I read the top sheet at arm's length. It was a receipt threatening me with all sorts of action if I failed to return the material. I signed it with the pen attached to the clip, thanked her, and started to gather up the files.

"Uh-uh. They stay here." A chin as solid as a doorstop jerked toward a laminate elbow–school desk in a corner.

I started to say that wouldn't do me any good, but her suspicion was already aroused; it would light up in the morning and hum at low power all night. I off-loaded the stack to the corner.

It didn't seem as if any local business could fill as many file folders as the Islamic State, but there were bundles of photos of Carl Fannon, derelict buildings getting ready to change hands, and Velocity's plush headquarters, taken at all angles and marked up for cropping. What they mostly didn't contain was any visual proof that Emil Haas existed. I've said he was camera shy; that was an understatement. He'd appeared on film about as often as Count Dracula. On the evidence he'd never traveled outside the country, so hadn't posed for a passport photo. I'd checked with Lansing:

The Secretary of State's office had no record of a driver's license in his name. He was God's gift to limousines, taxi, and Uber. I went through three folders before I saw an elbow in a houndstooth sleeve that might belong to him on the edge of yet another picture of Fannon shaking hands with some suit. The brains and conscience of the company was every bit the gray eminence he'd claimed to be, at home with his numbers and prognostications while the flashy other half sucked up the spotlight.

All of which made him look more guilty than he might have. Why go to such lengths to avoid cameras if you weren't planning to take it on the lam?

My eyes were watering and the smell of rubber cement was giving me a contact high when I finally hit pay dirt. I almost missed it; Fannon's barn-door grin front and center and hand resting on the shoulder of an East Indian in checked Armani might have been patched in from all the previous shots. I was about to toss it in the deadwood with the rest when I recognized the face of the man standing in the background and to the left, as noncommittal as his hands folded monk-fashion in front of him. His right ear was partially cut off by the frame, and black Sharpie lines directed the production staff to crop him out entirely, but it was a good likeness. I could spend a month down there and never find better.

I glanced over at the gatekeeper. She was reading her computer screen through a pair of glasses with tiger-striped rims. I closed the folder in front of me without making any noise and slid it onto the discard stack with one hand, blocking her view as I slipped the photo into an inside breast pocket.

Which, in case anyone wonders, is why I wear a suit every day.

The day was getting on, and so was I; but the nature of the establishment that made that ugly stationery available to its guests didn't offer much hope that the man who'd sent it was there for the long haul. A Syrian refugee who'd crawled through barbed wire, slept in a trench, and stowed away in a freezing luggage compartment would check out of the place in days, in search of better accommodations. That was management strategy, just like the uncomfortable seats in fast-food restaurants: Move 'em in, move 'em out. Dive that it was, it hadn't turned on the VACANCY sign in a decade. There were always a couple of rooms held in reserve for someone who'd fled to the Midwest for his health and liberty. The fact that it was currently named the Liberty Inn must have galled the authorities.

It was the Larkspur the first time I saw it, but it had changed names more often than an unpopular government project. The premise was that anyone familiar with its reputation might assume it was under new ownership; but even the Arab behind the registration desk had been there since before the first Gulf War, and his paychecks still came by way of an empty drop box in Omaha, en route from only the FBI knew where. It would be a party they could nab any time, but why throw away five more years investigating to find out who took his place?

The motel's new name was blocked out on a shield-shaped wooden sign facing the access road alongside I-96, with stars on a blue field at the top and vertical red-and-white stripes below. The color scheme had been applied to the wooden siding and outside staircases leading to the second-story porch, and the shake shingles and fancy coach lamps were new since my last visit. It all looked spruce enough to have cost plenty, but the material was cheap and the paint had all the indelibility of face powder. That gave the management the excuse to redo the place every three years, with meticulous bookkeeping to show that only the best quality went into the job. If the linens were laundered as thoroughly as the money that passed through the place, the Liberty Inn would be in Michelin.

The lobby had been redone too, along the Federal line, with star-spangled bunting on the windows, Colonial-type seating—flimsy-looking, but it wasn't as if anyone ever sat in it—and a gilded wooden bald eagle spreading its wings across the front of the desk. The Arab clerk showed no recognition as I crossed the Betsy Ross flag enameled on the floor tiles and gave him the friendly smile. He was handsome and dusky with his black hair in carefully unkempt curls and the promise of a splendidly Bedouin beard lurking just under the outer epidermis of his cheeks and chin. His blazer was tailored to resemble a Minuteman's tunic, blue with white facings on cuffs permanently turned back. He asked, in a deep voice without accent, if I had a reservation.

"Lay off, Hadaad. I'll stay here when the SEC comes after my Apple stock." I gave him a card anyway. He glanced at it and slid it into the slot in the desk top where he disposed of old registration cards. A shredder whined briefly. "I'm looking for a recent arrival."

He reached for the photograph I showed him, but I jerked it back before he could send it after my card.

He smiled at me. Some of that freshly washed cash had gone into the kind of dental work you see in dentists' billboards twelve feet wide. "Some trick. I guess it's no longer classified. Washington's shifted all its attention to terrorists, I guess."

"Huh?" I didn't think anything I heard in that building would stop me that cold.

"'Recent arrival.'" Did I just come in with a carload of figs?" Ignoring Emil Haas in the background, he pointed at the East Indian grinning at Carl Fannon. "Chacharan Dilawar. He owns the joint. Or he did before he sold it."

"Who'd he sell it to?" I asked; but I knew the answer.

Getting a look beyond the lobby was high on my Things to Do list that day, but there were thirty rooms and I'd made too many unsuccessful runs at those shredded registration cards to waste time trying. Hadaad had the eyes of an African eagle and an iron bladder; either that, or the brand of adult diapers issued by NASA. He never left the desk, or for that matter sat down.

The unofficially designated smoking area was the southeast corner of the empty lot beyond where the Dumpsters were parked, one of hundreds of chigger-hatcheries in the Renaissance City, with more being added every month. When I entered it the only occupant was a maintenance worker, a very tall, very thin man with dirty white hair and a strawberry mark that started at his hairline and dived down inside the collar of his green work shirt, sucking on a Virginia Slim.

I took up space beside him and tapped a Winston against the pack. "I thought that brand was for women."

He smoked silently for a moment, then cleared his throat, making no more noise than a jackhammer bouncing down the side of a scaffold. "Me, too, until a tough-guy crime writer came around a couple of years ago soaking up atmosphere. He gave me one. Smooth as the balls on a two-year-old."

I didn't know whether to chuckle at that one. He might have pictures on his personal computer.

We stood shoulder-to-shoulder like a couple of cons in the yard, poisoning our lungs with first- and secondhand smoke. After a little I took the photo from my pocket, folding Carl Fannon and Chacharan Dilawar to the back, and showed him Emil Haas. "Ever see this one in the motel?"

A blue eye floating in burst vessels drifted toward the picture, then back to the vacant space between where we were standing and the back of the building. "You a writer?"

"I can make my way through a postcard, but that's about all. I've been soaking up the atmosphere in this town so long I sweat it out my pores. I'm working with the cops on a missing-persons case. The guy's daughter wants him back."

"Reward?"

"Couple of hundred." If she balked at that I could make it up out of Fannon's advance.

"That ain't much."

I put away the picture. "You saw his suit. You don't pay for that kind of tailoring by spraying the cash all around town."

He'd burned the cigarette down to the filter. He plucked

it from between his lips, let it drop, mashed it into the dirt with a steel-tipped toe, and started back toward the motel.

To his back I said, "She might go three."

"And next week, then what?" he said without stopping or turning his head. "Rate this town's going, there won't be another maintenance job left after I'm canned."

Left alone, I watched a sheet of clouds dirtier than his hair unroll across the sky like an infield tarp, heard an approaching whoosh I knew well from hunting days before the pheasants ran out, and sprinted for the Dumpsters just as the rain swept across the lot with the force of a sandblaster. The drops were already bouncing up off hard earth and pattering my cuffs as I reached the shelter of the narrow pass-through under the second-story porch. A pair of women in gray housekeeping uniforms came down the open wooden steps, hooting at the sudden downpour with its rush of cool, iron-smelling air, and joined me, fishing packs out of their apron pockets.

I smiled at them, but said nothing. Squealers never come in sets. You have to get them alone. This pair burned their way through a butt apiece without even commenting on the rain, and when they went back upstairs trailing the last throatful of noxious gas I felt like Tom Hanks hanging out with his pal the basketball.

I was so busy watching the first flake of cheap paint separate itself from the siding I didn't realize I had company until a feminine voice with a guttural Eastern European accent asked me for a light. She must have come out the steel door marked STAFF ONLY NO ADMITTANCE on the far end of the pass-through, a small woman in her thirties with her hair pulled into a bun so tight her face shone like smooth plastic. She had a unibrow and a trace of moustache, and if a smile ever appeared under it, it was after the end of her shift.

I struck a match, shielding it from the damp wind with my palm, and set fire to the brown tube of tobacco stuck in a corner of her lips. She thanked me in that same deep voice and hugged herself. There were goose bumps on her bare arms.

"How you getting along with Velocity?" I asked.

"Yes?"

"The new owners."

A shoulder moved. She untangled her arms long enough to tap ash off her cigarette without taking it from her lips, then refolded them. "Is nothing change."

I showed her the picture. She paled a shade under the sheen.

"Police?"

"Friend."

"No."

I couldn't tell if she was arguing with me or didn't recognize Haas.

"He'd be new," I said. "His people are looking for him. A hundred dollars just for the room number."

"Nobody new but one. Not him."

"Can you describe the new guest?"

She got rid of more ash without removing the cigarette, then said something in a language that sounded like English played backwards.

"I don't speak Russian," I said.

"Is Romanian. It means cripple."

A tractor-trailer rig rattle-banged up the ramp to I-96, the Walter P. Chrysler Freeway, hiccuping up through its infinity of gears. The vibration made the soles of my feet itch. That was a fresh series of potholes in the making. After cars and undeveloped real estate, Detroit majors in shattered infrastructure. Japanese automakers come halfway around the world to make plaster-of-Paris molds for import to their proving grounds.

I looked down at the fresh cigarette smoldering between my fingers. I didn't remember ditching the last one, let alone lighting up another.

"What kind of cripple?"

"He limps."

"Lots of people limp. Could be just a sprain."

"One leg is false."

"You can tell that from just a limp?"

"Where I come from everybody limps. A broken bone is different from a clubfoot is different from a leg that is missing. The combine, the grain elevator, they have a mind of their own, and it is not always—charitable; this is a word?"

"Yes."

"Not in Romania." She rolled the *R* with a sort of snarl.

"Fair hair, medium build, about five-eleven, looks younger than he probably is?"

"Maybe. I do not see his hair. He wears a hat."

He never wore a hat except when he went incognito. His photo had run with his column when he had one and his face had appeared on cable and on the Internet. A porkpie or a ball cap can alter a look.

"Was he missing any fingers?"

"I do not look at hands checking in, only checking out, in case there is a tip."

"Southern accent?"

The tip of her cigarette glowed as she drew on it, thinking. She blew twin plumes of smoke out her nostrils, shook her head. "He says, 'Pardon me' when he slides past my cart in the hall. I can't tell from two words only."

He'd spent six months embedded in the Dixie Mafia without carrying away so much as a twang. I'd thrown her that one just to see if she was gussying up her story for the cash. "Which room?"

A pause while she threw another butt on the ground and replaced it from a cardboard box sporting a picture of a character in a spiked helmet and handlebars. The silence continued after I lit her up. I got the hint then. I took two fifties out of my wallet and held them up with the corners showing. They went into an apron pocket just short of giving me a paper cut.

"Sixteen. Corner room, second floor, end of the hall."

I was detective enough to find the room; they all bore shiny copper numbers. It remained to be seen whether I was detective enough to learn how Barry Stackpole had traced Emil Haas when I hadn't even told him I was looking for him.

TWENTY-ONE

This last was a philosophical problem, best worked out before a roaring fire with my feet in worn slippers steaming on the fender and a glass of cognac growing older and mustier in one hand. The first order of business was to get past Hadaad.

The homey look of the Liberty Inn was deceptive. Beyond the whitewashed wood and open porches skulked a state-of-the-art security system, complete with cameras, motion sensors, and cameras behind the cameras activated by body heat. More than in most hostels, the guests there were the most precious thing on the premises; one tip toward the feds in the MacNamara Building downtown to the present whereabouts of a Ten Most Wanted, and someone paid with his hide. The humble desk clerk earned close to the salary of any General Motors board member, but his golden parachute had a hole in it as big as the RICO Act. It led six feet down in the poured foundation of the Red Wings' new arena.

I was sixty feet away from Barry's room where the information the late Carl Fannon had paid me for was waiting;

not counting Emil Haas's and daughter Gwendolyn's retainers, however cut-rate. A five-minute walk any other day, but today it was the 500 K. Hemingway had said something along those lines while revisiting the scene of his wounding during the First World War; thirty-some yards that had taken more than a year and 75,000 casualties to cover.

The Romanian housekeeper gave me some hope. The rustle of the two fifties in her apron pocket whenever she shifted her weight from one foot to the other had thawed the snowcaps of the Carpathians. She offered me one of her cigarettes. It was a Turkish knockoff, oval-shaped to fool the uneducated eye, but probably Nigerian in origin, laced with lead and toxic runoff from some off-shore operation based in New Jersey. A veteran could burn a thousand of them without effect, but six puffs by a pampered American could put him in Intensive Care.

I accepted it, of course. You never turn down hospitality on the job, at least not on my job. When I put flame to it, it burned a third of the way down its length and ignited the tobacco—or whatever it was stuffed with—in a pyrotechnics display of sparks and glowing bits of metal, probably steel shavings. I tried to exhaust as much of it out the corner of my mouth opposite the one where it rested. I preferred to fill my lungs with homegrown poison.

"Is there a back way up to the second floor?" My throat felt tight; the stuff corrugated the lining.

She drew the last of her latest to the floor of her lungs, took it from her lips, contemplated what was left, took one last puff, and let it fall to the ground. A gust of smoke escaped her mouth.

"You have another suit, yes?" She evaluated mine with the gimlet eye of an Odessa tailor.
"Yes. But this is my best."
"Too bad."

I'd done worse, but not since Saigon fell.

Local codes had mandated an air shaft through the center of the construction, to supply ventilation to the second floor. Architecturally speaking, it was a hollow square leading from ground level to the roof, furnishing a handy place for the incessant parade of renovators to dispose of unrecyclable waste. Piles of broken Sheetrock, drywall, and acoustical ceiling lay at the base of a rectangular shaft broken only by ledges of mortar squeezed out between two-by-fours. They made convenient handholds: for Spider-Man. For a somewhat-past middle-aged detective, they represented stripping out of his suitcoat, frequent deep breaths, and disgruntled spiders.

At the end of ten minutes I hoisted myself onto the second-story walkway by my elbows and looked up, square into the lens of a camera mounted directly above the shaft. I climbed to my feet, listening for the thunder of jackboots on the stairs, and when five more minutes had passed in peace I took a closer look at the camera. There were no cables connected to it.

Romanian Annie might have told me it was a dummy; but it would probably have cost my dead client another hundred.

The boards creaked underfoot, but there was nothing I could do about that. If Hadaad had orders to make sure

Barry didn't leave his room and no one came to rescue him, I just had to move fast. I took out the stiff vinyl strip ostensibly designed to reinforce my wallet, but before slipping the latch I tried knocking, and damn if the peg-legged rascal didn't swing open the door and aim a Taser at my heart. He'd probably heard me coming ever since I started up the air shaft.

TWENTY-TWO

Bar's open." Barry laid the Taser on a table inside the door. "On the dresser."

This was three drawers of printed wood grain supporting a seventeen-inch flat screen, the usual tray, ice bucket, and plastic cups, and a square bottle of Gentleman Jack.

"You didn't get this from room service." I stripped the cellophane off a cup and floated two cubes from the bucket. "You can call a lot of attention to yourself checking in with your luggage in a paper sack." There was nothing hanging in the doorless closet and not even a backpack in sight.

"I haven't checked into a hotel or motel in ten years, and I've stayed in plenty. I slipped Lawrence of Arabia downstairs a fifty to leave his little box of cards under the desk." He stretched out on the bed and folded his hands behind his head. He was in shirtsleeves, slacks, and one sock. The other foot was titanium, shaped like an electric iron and attached by a socket to a metal rod. In the time I'd known him he'd gone from spruce to fiberglass to the stuff they use to build the space shuttle.

There was a talk show on TV, one of those where the guests make their point by throwing chairs at each other. The volume was low, but made enough murmur to keep anyone from following our conversation with his ear to the door. That was an everyday precaution for Barry.

"Hadaad's selling himself short," I said. "The going rate among the housekeeping staff is a hundred."

"The way I hear it, you've been scattering C-notes all over town like grass seed. You must have a printing press in the garage."

"Quit kidding, chum. I'd farm out all my work to you if I didn't think I'd be watching it on the next news cycle. You know damn well who I'm working for or you wouldn't be here, sitting on my latest lead."

"You could have saved us both a lot of trouble if you'd trusted me in the first place. I worked my way backwards from Peaceable Shore. It holds the deed to this place. I filed all the details behind my firewall when it changed hands. You think I don't keep track of what happens to the Liberty?"

"When did you make the connection?"

"Don't worry, it was after we spoke. I had to check it out before I said anything. One bum steer can ruin a relationship."

"You left every sign of an unplanned disappearance."

"I'm glad you noticed. Once too many times I followed standard procedure and told a colleague where I was going. He sold me out, which is the reason I buy one shoe at a time. I can't trust anyone with what I'm doing; not even you,

Amos. Hell, there are days when I don't confide in myself. But only an idiot plunges half-cocked into an investigation connected with a murder. If I stepped out unannounced, leaving my door open, someone—maybe the UPS man who delivers author's copies of my books—will put my face on a milk carton."

He rolled onto one shoulder, snared a can of salted almonds off the nightstand, and lay back, prying off the plastic lid.

"I'm glad it was you," he said, "for what it's worth. Sorry about that trusting crack."

"Yeah. We should take up a line of work where we can depend on each other. Maybe the trapeze."

I held up the bottle and sloshed it. He shook his head, munching. "I was saving it for you. Nuts are instant energy. I ride the wagon when I'm working."

"I should too." I made myself uncomfortable in a Naugahyde recliner and drank. I'm not a bourbon fan; it isn't strong enough for rocket fuel and it isn't sweet enough to pour on a waffle. But any Jack in a storm. It shinnied up my spine and started gnawing at my gray cells. "So what'd you get, apart from a suitcase stuffed with bottles of conditioning shampoo?"

"In this dump you bring your own. You first. I know you're working for Velocity, but I don't know which half."

"Take your pick. Either way you're right."

"Strictly speaking there's only one choice, with Fannon in the hospitality suite in the Wayne County Morgue."

"Who says that rules him out?"

He nodded. "I forgot. When it comes to clients you don't

discriminate over whether they have a pulse. How much of the dead man's money have you burned through so far?"

"Not much, in the greater scheme of things. These days I have to beat clients away with a blackjack. You haven't figured out the riddle yet."

"What's to figure out? You found another moneybags, this one with moving parts."

I swirled the contents of my plastic cup, but the ice didn't make that crisp clink I associate with the rest of the pleasures of boozing. It doesn't have to be cut crystal; a glass jar would do. "I'm all about the money. That's why I've got a pack of gum on layaway at the IGA. Just now I'm lugging around a cool forty bucks in cash, courtesy of Emil and Gwendolyn Haas. At this rate I'm going to have to open an account in Switzerland."

"What are you doing for all this plunder?"

"You can't use it, Barry. Not now, and maybe not ever."

He put the lid back on the can. "So it's what we talked about?"

"I hope not; but until I can swear it isn't, I'm sitting on top of a thousand-gallon tank of gasoline, playing with matches."

"Okay. But when you can swear it isn't, it's mine."

So I told him.

About Fannon hiring me to find Emil Haas to avoid queering the deal over the Sentinel Building, Haas slipping me twenty to meet him in that same location, and the twenty I got from Gwendolyn to locate her father and clear him of suspicion in his partner's murder;

About my adventures with three outfits called Peaceable Shore, all of which offered possibilities—even the one that

had closed—but none more promising than the others. Drugs or human misery or sex for hire, take your pick;
About Lieutenant Child.

"He's using you for bait," Barry said.

"Sure he is. When a cop tells you he's not ambitious, you can bet he's got his eye on Everest."

"Man, you do more all day than I do before breakfast. All I have to show for my stay in this slick rattrap is the name of the person Velocity's been fronting for all this time."

I rolled the cup between my palms, watching the ice lose its sharp corners. So far I'd had only the one sip. "What's this lesson in investigative journalism going to cost me?"

"This one's on the house. I can't use it anyway; I knew that when we made our deal. I've got as much stake in nailing this particular party as everyone else in civilization. I told Haas to write his daughter, using Liberty stationery. I knew if she showed it to anyone, it'd be you. With Daddy's name all over the police news, she wouldn't go to them, and the young ladies of her set don't have any snoopers on speed-dial. She'd have gotten your name from his office."

"I'd offer you a partnership, if there were enough work for two. I couldn't get much out of Brita Palmerston there."

"If you got anything, you got more than I did. The receptionist told me she went out for lunch and didn't come back. But I was just touching base. After that I talked to Gwendolyn. I didn't have to play pig-in-a-poke with her like you did. My partnership is with the First Amendment. The cops don't like it, but I don't have to tell them anything about my sources, even sources who are the subject of an all-points-bulletin. I read Haas's note."

I sat forward. "You found him?"

He gave me his baggy grin, put the lid back on the can of nuts, wiped his hands with a cheesy motel tissue, reached above the maple headboard, and rapped the can against the wall. A poorly set floor tile creaked under a footstep, the bathroom door opened, and Emil Haas stepped out.

TWENTY-THREE

He was dressed more casually than the one time we'd met—almost elaborately so—in a plain blue shirt, dark gray slacks, and black loafers, all screaming some Mom-and-Pop store where the merchandise was more expensive than in a big-box outlet, without any difference in quality. Had he shown his infamous face in Walmart or Meijer or any mall in the metropolitan area, the security footage would have been on TV and the Net inside an hour.

He was a big man still, but the way he stood, shriveled inside himself, lessened the effect, and the absence of careful tailoring showed off his physical defects; he wasn't noticeably overweight, but when it came to even a modest spare tire, cheap beltless trousers weren't made with flattery in mind.

I put aside my drink and climbed out of the recliner. "Next time you go underground, don't try so hard to be invisible. If I just got back from Mars and hadn't seen a paper or TV or been online, I'd still report you to the cops as a suspicious person."

He blinked a little, completing the image he projected. With his pale curly hair and Elmer's Glue-All complexion, he could have passed for albino. It was ironic; in ordinary circumstances he was the original Mr. Cellophane, seldom noticed and instantly forgotten. On the lam, he stuck out like a snowy owl in a flock of crows.

"Mr. Stackpole made me well aware of the conspicuous figure I cut," he said in that shallow tone. It made you want to lean closer to hear him. Maybe that was his secret, what had attracted a charismatic character like Carl Fannon to him in the first place. From across a room, anyone polite enough to address him in conversation would look as if he were hanging on to every word he said. "You must understand I've had no practice."

I looked at Barry, sitting up in bed now with the can of nuts in his lap, tapping the plastic lid and turning it into a toy bongo. "Where'd you two crazy kids meet?"

"Right in this room. He was checking out as I was checking in—figuratively speaking. His name wasn't in Hadaad's box any more than mine, but room sixteen was in the active file, the only blank card there. There were always at least a few under the old management. You boys threw away a gold mine when you canceled company policy regarding unregistered guests," he told Haas.

"Carl said the same thing, but I said we'd make many times that legitimately by razing the place and putting up a professional building. He said, 'It'd take us three years to recoup the investment. Meanwhile the place is bringing in as much as the Hilton, and most of it under the IRS radar.' I'd suspected his moral compass was out of whack, but it was then I decided to follow his paper trail."

"What took you so long?" I asked. "You two have been buying up the city for years."

"He always made a good pitch, and we cleaned up by flipping the property or renovating it and leasing space. I created a Frankenstein there. When we started out, he wanted to invest in sites in New York, Chicago, and L.A. I told him everyone did that, buying high when the local economy was booming and selling low when it went bust, when it should be the other way around. I reminded him of all those high-rise office buildings that sprang up in Houston like mushrooms when oil was selling at sixty dollars a barrel; when it dropped below thirty, the owners were offering three months' occupancy rent-free to fill the empty space. In Detroit, you can buy a row of abandoned houses for a dollar apiece and back taxes, an empty industrial plant for less than the cost of a loft in Manhattan, and turn them over three years later for a million. When we started doing that, I saw no reason to question why the money came in so fast, or where the initial investment was coming from. I parked my nose in the black column and ignored the red as a temporary situation."

Barry said, "You can get in a lot of trouble not asking the questions you don't want to know the answers to."

"I didn't think to ask the questions. When Cecil Fish and his cronies started accusing Velocity of fronting for foreign interests, I started. Carl kept ducking the issues I kept bringing up, so I opened my own inquiries outside the office. We were right in the middle of the Sentinel Building deal when I found out about Peaceable Shore." He turned to me. The blinking stopped. "That's when I missed our appointment with the owners and went to see you instead. Things had gotten to the point where it was too dangerous to keep the secret to myself."

"Walker told you when you came to his office you'd saved a lot of people a lot of time and money. You could have saved a lot more if you'd said your piece there."

"A lot more," I said. "Like your partner's life."

"I told you I didn't trust speaking out in a strange place."

I said, "You've got a half-interest in almost every empty hulk in town. You picked the Sentinel for what, sentimental reasons?"

"Hardly. It's closed to the public, the workers go home at five, and I had a key. Also the building was germane to the conversation. It was during our negotiations to buy it I found out just who we were dealing with. My meeting with you would be brief: One name."

"I was there. Where were you?"

"Across the street in the first doorway I came to after I left the basement. I saw you talk to the derelict in the alley, then go inside."

"You left an Easter egg behind."

He nodded, and went on nodding. As large as his brain cavity was, it still wasn't big enough for a bobblehead. "I thought it must have been you who found Carl, though no one said or wrote anything about who it was.

"No," he said, shaking his head now, "I didn't put him there, but when I found the vault door was shut and discovered it was locked, I decided to get out. We'd left specific instructions to the workmen to remove the door to avoid just that kind of mishap. I'd have opened it myself if I knew anything about it. I suspected someone was trapped inside, a natural reaction; and I couldn't afford to be found there under those circumstances. I panicked. I can't deny it. Still, I don't suppose I could have saved Carl in any case. Unless the police gave the media false information?" He looked like a man begging for scraps.

"He'd been dead for hours." I scooped my cup off the lamp table and drank. The ice was gone, diluting the bourbon. It tasted like one of those spiked lemonades kids drink when they think they're boozing. "I'm no more safe cracker than you are. The lock let go while I was standing in front of it. You wouldn't know anything about that."

"Good God. I didn't see a timer. Do you think someone set it to open while I was there?"

"That was the first thing I thought; only I thought I was supposed to be the patsy. But if someone tipped the cops to stumble over one or the other of us red-handed, the message got lost. They didn't show until after I told your office manager not to expect Fannon to check in from Beijing."

Barry had stopped thumping the can in favor of shaking it and rattling the almonds inside. "Not so far-fetched. There are nine-one-one operators I wouldn't trust to remember to pick up my dry cleaning."

"Maybe. I'm still on the list for reporting the body late and not directly to the authorities. Maybe whoever put him in storage and set the clock thought that would happen. Or that I'd pretend I was never there and then they'd have something on me."

"My God." Haas came the rest of the way into the room and lowered himself into the recliner. "And I thought legitimate business was Machiavellian."

"Forget Machiavelli," said Barry. "He was an *Our Gang* kid compared to Charlotte Sing."

I finished my drink in one steady draught and set it down with a bang. "There it is, damn it. I was hoping no one would mention the name. Now it's real."

Outside, a Volt or a Tesla or something equally electric and quiet hummed down the interstate. That's how silent the room had gotten.

Emil Haas broke it. "I didn't even know who Charlotte Sing was until I ran a computer check on all the possible synonyms for Peaceable Shore. And I'd never heard of Peaceable Shore until I found it on Carl's. He thought by erasing it from his hard drive, he'd eradicated it. He forgot I got my start designing programs. I traced Peaceable Shore to Pacific Rim. The images that followed were hellish. That company managed to turn terrorism into a commercial enterprise. And it was run by a woman."

"She's not a woman," I said. "She's a pandemic in Prada."

Barry said, "I've been underestimating Cecil Fish. His computer guru must have found out about it the same way you did."

I was staring at Haas. "How could you not know who Madam Sing was? Six months before the North Koreans reported her arrest, sure, but six weeks after that she was *Time*'s Person of the Year, edging out Sheikh Killabuncha-christians."

"If I came across her at all, I dismissed it as not important to Velocity. Had I known my own partner was financing us with funds provided by an international criminal, I'd have done the homework I've been doing since I found out about Peaceable Shore."

"She's dead. You said it yourself, Barry. They hanged her in Pyongyang for every count in sixty-three countries."

Barry scowled at his can of nuts and threw it in a corner. "I know all Asians are supposed to look alike, but she outdid herself when she cast her substitute. I even did a face match on that shot somebody bootlegged onto the Net. It was grainy, and there's bound to be distortion when a neck is broken at the end of a length of coarse Tibetan hemp, but it rang a gong from every angle."

I said, "It was probably one of the human-trafficking cases in her prostitution ring, helped along by plastic surgery. For someone who started out as a slave in a cathouse, she wasn't above running the same racket. She'd smuggled drugs and human organs and committed murder personally, just to keep in practice. Add it to her tab."

"*Isn't* above running the same racket," Barry said. "You keep referring to her in the past tense."

"Maybe if I do she will be."

Haas was watching me. "You talk as if you've met."

"He shattered her hand the last time." Barry's tone was funereally low. "It's how she wound up in custody to begin with."

"We've met," I said, as if he hadn't spoken. "One time or a hundred. Never is too much. Just why she doesn't pick on another city every time she comes back—it keeps me up nights. Urban blight, wholesale corruption, and the worst homicide rate in the country aren't punishment enough. We have to have Charlotte Sing. Why not the apocalypse?"

"Haas gave you the answer a minute ago. She told you the last time her bank account was hovering down around a hundred million. These days you need a couple of billion just to put the destruction of western culture on the table. Detroit is the only place in America where you can gobble up real estate with pocket change and turn it into serious cash. Whatever she's got cooking this time, we know where she's getting her case dough.

"And Amos," Barry added, "*you're* here. That's got to be another fortune in her cookie."

TWENTY-FOUR

That's the second racist remark you've made in as many minutes," said Haas.

Barry said, "She's a race unto herself. *Homo maligno*. Ever since her G.I. father sold her into slavery she's had a hate on for everything west of the prime meridian."

"I suppose that's understandable."

"As much as shooting up a playground full of children because your own kid gave you grief," I said. "She's the most dangerous animal in the world: a deranged genius with a wallet the size of the Pentagon."

Barry recrossed his arms behind his head. "Intellectually gifted, check; crazy, definitely. But she didn't just pluck her stand-in on the scaffold off the street in Seoul. The search for a viable candidate would have taken months or years, and a series of cosmetic procedures with healing time in between at least as long. Notwithstanding the primitive methods of North Korean physicians, the sample they provided of the executed woman's DNA managed to satisfy the United Nations and the World Court. It was Sing's, of course: She supplied it. But she had to grease wheels, maybe all the way to the presidential palace. The compound fractures in the right hand matched Sing's old X-rays, which means her double had to sit still for an artist with a bludgeon. That's a chunk of change. My guess is she's so close to rock bottom she couldn't raise a fleet of private jets without a loan."

"So whatever she's got in mind for what she's making through Velocity, it's on hold till her checks clear."

"Made." Haas gripped the recliner's arms. "Not making. I'm stopping payment on all checks and declaring a moratorium on all accounts payable until our bookkeeping staff can sort out the legitimate investors from the rest."

I dealt myself a cigarette, frowned at the smoke detector in the corner of the ceiling, and cradled it unlit in the permanent niche in my lower lip. "You can't declare anything while you're a fugitive from justice. You need to turn yourself in while your *detecting* staff sorts out Ms. Fu Manchu from the rest of the population."

"How do I know she won't try to railroad me into a murder conviction? If she's capable of buying off a foreign government, framing one U.S. citizen—"

"Even psychos can reason," I said. "There's no percentage in it for her, and she hasn't the time. It's obvious she had Fannon killed to stop up the leak you were investigating. Without him, there's no link to her except two words on his computer that wouldn't hold up in court; if she cares about courts at all after what she just pulled. I wasted a day on three Peaceable Shores in this area alone. Also she probably wasn't within ten thousand miles of the crime scene when it happened."

Barry said, "Let's hope."

"Even if she was, she's got the best alibi in the world: She's officially dead. Whoever was at the end of the strings, if he's caught and he fingers her, won't be believed. Assuming he knows who hired him. If she tipped her hand to him, she's slipped a lot."

"Which based on what she's got going with Velocity isn't likely," said Barry. "It's a simple plan, and brilliant. If Fish or any of your other enemies manages to make any of his accusations stick, she's managed to shift the blame to China. You can damn well bet if Peaceable Shore ever surfaces, so will a direct link to the People's Republic."

"Do it," I told Haas. "I'll drive you to Homicide and let you off at the curb. You can walk right up to the desk and do the citizenship thing."

"And after you let me off, what will you be doing?"

"Earning the fee your daughter gave me. Proving you innocent."

He stood and scooped the receiver off the phone on the nightstand. "I'll call my lawyer. He can do the driving."

While he was speaking with whoever picked up, Barry took me into a corner. "Where'll you start?"

"Off the record?"

"Come on."

"Sorry. Old habit. Downtown. To talk to a man named Frank about a package of wieners."

Richard, Cecil Fish's pudgy, not-as-young-as-he-looked assistant, kept me on hold two minutes while I listened to a campaign plug for his boss. He wasn't openly running for anything, but he had a collection of area city officials and county executives lined up, each with a foot in the door when it came time for endorsements. Just what he had on them was anyone's guess.

"Sorry about that, Mr. Walker. What can I do for you?"

"Sweet of you to offer. I was wondering if you'd had any luck running down that party we talked about last time."

"Running d—? Oh, you mean locating. No, no one seems to know where he's gone. I don't mind telling you the experience opened my eyes to the plight of the homeless. What we need is someone—"

"What we've got is the Salvation Army, Forgotten Harvest, the VA, Mother Waddles, and more churches than a bishop could shake his stick at. I heard the pitch while you were slitting envelopes and answering more important calls. Thank you so much."

I hit END. On the other side of my windshield, a troupe of yellow school buses crawled along I-96, heading for some soccer game. I'd waited until I got to the parking lot before calling. I trusted Barry's "off the record," but there was no sense sharing trade secrets with my client.

I was relieved. I'd only thrown Frank to Fish in return for Peaceable Shore. The derelict outside the Sentinel Building wasn't of use to me then. Had I known I'd be doing Homicide's job, I'd have rolled him up and tucked him in my sock. If Richard had gotten to him first, he'd be ruined as a witness. All it takes to make a street survivor clam up is an amateur asking the wrong questions the wrong way. As it was, just pumping the refrigerator-box crowd for his whereabouts had probably driven him deeper underground. When someone you habitually overlook suddenly draws your attention, his first reaction is flight.

But that was okay. I know all the flight patterns.

I drove to the city offices, now named the Coleman A. Young building by someone with a short memory. It's from the Lego school of architecture: nineteen charmless stories attached to a box squatting at the busiest intersection in town. When they forgot to put windows on the side facing Woodward—just the city's main street—a local sculptor erected a Neanderthal there in tarnished bronze and called it the *Spirit of Detroit*.

Pontius Quick took up space in an office two floors down from the top of the tower. Its size matched its view of downtown; it was a square trinket box on the building's blank side. He was in his late sixties, cinnamon-colored, with white hair and beard, both buzzed close, and wore a green uniform in solidarity with the army he commanded: employees of the Department of Public Works and the Health Department assigned to rodent control.

City Hall is too busy counting violent crimes to estimate the number of rats in residence. The rule of thumb says cities have twice as many rats as people. The last census fixed the population at just under a million, so if you prefer your glass half full, the vermin problem improves every time someone decamps to the suburbs.

"Who's winning, Ponch?" I shook his big hand and sat down in the metal folding chair facing his desk, a pressboard item no bigger than you'd find in a cubicle but too big for the room. On it he'd arranged family pictures in a half-circle facing him. There always seemed to be a new one whenever I visited. The Quicks were multiplying almost as fast as his quarry.

"Oh, I expect real results real soon. Got me a councilman's

nephew on staff worked out a formula to calculate the strength of the enemy: Just count the legs and divide by four." He jerked a thumb over his shoulder at a framed PhotoShop picture of himself grinning in a safari outfit with a rifle on his shoulder and one foot propped up on the carcass of a rat the size of a dump truck. "I sent him up to Greektown, where they're redoing the casino, with a calculator. You know every time they swing that big iron ball a couple thousand rats come scrambling out of the rubble. It's like busting the world's worst piñata."

"I saw a bunch the other day marching out of Toyota. You know what people say about when they desert."

"The gents on the top floor just authorized another sixty grand for poison. I don't know why we don't just pipe in water from Flint. What brings you down to City, Amos? Going back into the public sector, human race got too much for you?"

"God, no." I rapped on his desk, not that there was enough real wood in it for luck. "I threw down the badge, just like Gary Cooper. I won't pick it up. You still running that program you learned from Chairman Mao?"

"Hell, yes. Doing bidness with some of the finest folks in town. We're under budget third straight year. I got to cook the books up instead of down so's they don't cut my allowance. You volunteering?"

Pontius Quick had come up with an extermination plan so simple it was no wonder no one else in government had ever thought of it. No one else, that is, except Mao Tse-tung, who wrote a law requiring each one of Communist China's billion citizens to turn in a daily quota of swatted flies to his local Communist Party headquarters or be fined.

Detroiters don't pay fines—they don't even pay bills for city services—but Quick had been commended by the mayor for shaking loose a quarter for every man, woman, and child living in a shelter or on the streets for each dead rat delivered for inspection, relieving the crisis and helping the unfortunate at the same time. "Killing two rats with one stone," as he put it.

"I'm only after one rat, Ponch. I'm hoping to catch it through one of your irregulars. You've got their names on file, right?"

"First names and nicknames, mostly. Some of 'em been on the skids so long they don't remember the ones they was born with. Tally's got to match with what leaves the dump station, and each catch goes into a box with the name of who brought it in. One of the bugs I had to work out in the beginning was they'd go around to the Dumpster and come back in with carcasses we already counted and paid for."

"Like deposit bottles. When I was a kid I'd get two cents a pop from the party store, then go back around to the storage room and grab another load."

"Dating yourself. It's a dime now, and they lock up the bottles like government gold. No rat goes into the incinerator till it's been counted twice and paid for once."

"What about locations?"

"Oh, we stopped keeping 'em in the Dumpster overnight. Some folks are sensitive about smell."

"I mean the homeless people."

He squinted one eye. "What part of 'homeless' don't you understand?"

"Give me a break, for past associations."

I hated to draw that card. Five years back I'd sprung his

granddaughter from a junior high school expulsion for bringing her great-grandfather's captured German Luger to show-and-tell.

"'No tolerance,'" he snarled now. "I was brought up tolerant. What's your boy's handle?"

"Frank."

He didn't stir. "Narrows it down."

"He put the arm on me for the price of a package of wieners. Franks, he called them. Some joke."

"No help. Oscar Mayer's the new cuppa coffee." He made a noodling gesture with the fingers of one hand.

"The one time I saw him he had on one of those canvas vests with lots of pockets, like fishermen wear."

"They change clothes sometimes. Some of 'em even use soap, which is more than I can say for a couple of people in this building got bigger offices than mine."

"He has a tattoo on his chest."

"My brother's twins got pineapples on their butt-cheeks, and they ain't never been to Hawaii. I don't mean to be difficult. I got a meeting with the mayor today and a rabies specialist to interview: Set 'em up in that order in case Hizzoner bites me."

"The tat's a reasonable likeness of the *Edmund Fitzgerald*."

"Well, hell. They must pay you by the hour." He had a slim computer monitor on the corner of his desk. He spun it to face him and struck some keys hunt-and-peck. "Frank Nelson. Worked as a deckhand for McLouth Steel ten years—two on the *Fitzgerald*, by God—walked away from the navy after Desert Storm. Washington don't bother with peacetime deserters anymore, so why should I? Hangs his hat, when he's got one, in the shelter next to Annunciation on Lafayette."

"That's just a couple of blocks from where we met."

"They got rails and they run on 'em. What bidness you got with him?"

"Couple of questions. I saw a rat in a place near where we met, that's why I thought of him. He may have seen something connected with the job I'm on. He's not in any trouble that I know of."

"Just don't bend him. He brings in more carcasses than anyone else on the East Side. I got him lined up for this year's James Clavell Award. Comes with a six-month supply of food stamps. He can invite all his colleagues in for a wienie roast."

"Who's James Clavell?"

He smiled, showing off the city's premium dental plan. "He wrote *King Rat*."

TWENTY-FIVE

You've seen it in movies, read about it in books: the big bare room, divided into iron bedsteads with their legs stuck in coffee cans filled with kerosene to discourage roaches; maybe stern signs warning residents not to spit on the floor. But roaches are rare in Michigan and spitting's optional even if smoking is not. The homeless shelter next door to the Annunciation Greek Orthodox cathedral was built along the lines of a YMCA, partitioned into private rooms with comfortable beds, reading lamps on stands, and simple but sturdy cabinets for clothes, complete with plastic hangers. Throw in a TV and a bottle of Scotch and for me it was home sweet home.

The majordomo was a sturdy party of indeterminate age—and for that matter sex—in a smock, sweatpants, and canary-yellow Crocs, leaning on a cane with four sturdy tips, who met me in an eight-foot-square foyer paved with sturdy linoleum and painted in sturdy beige. Our city is constantly tearing itself down and putting up nothing in its place; but its homeless shelters are as solid as the Coliseum.

The creature had a stack of clean towels folded over one forearm. I tucked my card into a terry fold, faceup.

"I'm looking for a man named Frank Nelson. Social visit."

"Are you of the faith?" The voice was a contralto, if it was feminine. Tenor if not. I flipped a mental coin and it came down female.

"Do I have to be to see Frank?"

She shifted the towels to the other arm. "Are you carrying a weapon?"

"No. Should I be?"

"I'm going to have to ask you to leave."

"Let's start over." I got out my license folder and showed her the honorary sheriff's star. "He's not in any trouble. He might be a witness in a police case."

I spoke quietly, but two men got up from a bench just inside the door, gathered up their tattered bundles, and left.

"Please keep your voice low. The police aren't exactly popular here."

"What about Frank?"

"We don't ask them their names."

"He's got a tattoo of a shipwreck on his chest."

"Last room, end of the hall. Take this to him, please." She separated a plain white towel from the stack and held it out.

The rooms were separated by painted plywood, smudged with greasy telephone numbers and the odd phallic cartoon. They were open to the aisle. My hot dog man lay on a rollaway bed with an army blanket folded at the foot, a copy of *National Geographic* spread facedown on his stomach. It was hot in the building, despite window fans humming throughout. The fisherman's vest hung on the back of a plastic deck chair, giving me a clear view of the doomed ore carrier decorating his hairless chest. It wasn't moving.

I didn't linger long.

I found the woman with the towels, hanging them on rails attached to the partitions.

"Wouldn't he see you?" she asked.

"Couldn't. Is there a phone? I left my cell in the car."

"Is it a local call?"

"Nine-one-one. Someone smothered him with a pillow."

I didn't think Lieutenant Child had missed his regular barber's appointment. More likely whoever had touched him up that day had been better with the brush. His collar was free of clipped hairs, but he smelled like a fresh-squeezed lime. He had on a flat cap with a plaid to match his suit, and damned if he didn't uncover his head in the presence of the dead man. The woman from the medical examiner's office was already at work with her tool kit, which included a temporal thermometer she passed over his forehead and a little tape recorder. "Ninety-two-point one. At a guess, he died within the hour." She was talking to the gadget.

The pillow lay where I'd found it, next to his head with a dent in it the size of his face. Bits of lint from the case clung to his stubble. His eyes were two white semicircles, the irises rolled all the way back, and his mouth was frozen in a silent scream.

"And nobody saw nothing," Child said. "How's that?"

I said, "Only reason anyone saw me was I asked for him. Killers do their own looking."

"How'd you know to look here?"

"DPW. Frank was a champion rat-catcher."

"What else was he?"

"A possible witness in the Fannon murder."

"Based on what?"

I took a deep breath and told him how we'd met.

"I'm just learning about this now why?"

"At the time I didn't know what was waiting for me in the basement. Later it slipped my mind."

"What jogged your memory?"

"Cecil Fish. I traded him Frank for that Peaceable Shore tip I told you about."

"You fingering Fish?"

"Much as I'd like to, this isn't his style. I believed his assistant when he said he didn't have any luck finding Frank."

"He said this when?"

I told him.

"You're just a busy little bee, aren't you? In too much of a hurry to stop and clue me in on my own goddamn investigation."

"It wasn't my investigation when we spoke."

"What do you think Frank saw?"

"Maybe nothing. Maybe whoever went in that building and came out before I showed up."

"What makes it your investigation all of a sudden?"

"I'm working for Gwendolyn Haas to clear her father of the Fannon kill."

"I thought you were working on Fannon's dime."

"That was then. On this case all I have to do is stand still and the clients come wrapping themselves around my ankles like old sports sections."

"Funny thing. Haas showed up in my office a little while

ago with his lawyer, saying he wanted to do the same thing. You wouldn't know anything about that."

"I suggested it a couple of hours ago when we ran into each other in the Liberty Inn. I was going to tell you all about it after I talked to Frank. One of the reasons I came down here was to try to persuade him to go to you with what he knew."

"What brought you to the Liberty?"

"Just a hunch. It's where all the two-legged rats in the city wind up sooner or later."

Gwendolyn wouldn't have thanked me for telling him she'd gotten a note from Haas on Liberty stationery. I didn't know Child well enough to trust him not to slap her with a sheltering rap. I didn't know any cop well enough for that, including cops I'd known for thirty years.

"While I'm at it, tell Lieutenant Stonesmith she can stop looking for Barry Stackpole. I stumbled over him in Haas's room. He took off on his own. No foul play involved."

"So you say. It's so foul in here I could throw up, and I'm not talking about the stiff on the bed." He started patting his pockets. "You're under arrest, Walker. Withholding evidence to start. Got a Miranda card?" he asked the medical examiner.

"Why should I? I don't have any authority to arrest anyone. You've been watching too many episodes of *CSI*."

"Well, shit. You know your way around County," he told me. "What they said last time still goes." He reached under his coattail and jangled loose a pair of handcuffs.

Checking into Holding in the old Third Precinct was something I could cross off my bucket list. I'd spent enough time

in the cage at 1300 to use it as my voting address, but that
was before a chain of corrupt and inept mayors had let the
place go to the birds and the beasts of the field. Homicide
had been in those digs long enough to wear out that invigo-
rating new-hoosegow smell, but the bars had a fresh coat of
whitewash and the beige-painted walls weren't yet scribbled
over with the legacies left by former occupants. There was
no steel grid to protect the bulb, but the LED fixture behind
the opaque pebbled panel in the ceiling was too high for a
Pistons center to reach. The toilet had a lid and the trian-
gular corner sink drained like sixty.

The bed was another story. Recently bankrupt cities don't
go to Art Van's for new furniture when they move offices.
I was pretty sure I'd used this one before, and my tired old
muscles confirmed it. They hadn't even bothered to change
the walnuts in the stuffing.

Jails are quiet, whatever you've read in books or seen on
TV. The cell to my right was empty, the mattress rolled up
at one end on naked metal slats, and my neighbor on the left
slept more or less peacefully, making a little "pah" sound
every time he exhaled. Sleeping's the best way to pass the
time in the can once you've committed all the graffiti to
memory. You don't even have to be sleepy: You just close
your eyes and pretend you've got the flu.

When Lieutenant Child to the dark tower came, accom-
panied by a uniformed officer, I was dreaming about hunting grizzlies in Alaska. I'd never been to Alaska, had never
gotten any closer to a bear in the wild than *Animal Planet*,
and nothing I'd been exposed to lately was even slightly re-
lated to what I dreamt. It was an episode from *Sergeant
Preston of the Yukon*, dredged up from childhood. You know

you're past middle age when your brain's too far gone to process anything but stock footage. The rattle of the officer's key in the lock woke me.

"Man, you were out," Child said. "Must be them fine linen sheets."

"I just now dozed off. I think there's a pea under the mattress." I swung my feet to the floor and scratched my grouty scalp.

Someone cleared his throat. I looked up. There was a second man with him, six-and-a-half-feet high with hair as sleek and as close to his head as a bathing cap. The color scheme he wore was the same as his office on the nosebleed floor of the Capital One Building in Southfield, gray gabardine on yellow silk with a steel-gray necktie. He had the distracting habit of blinking constantly, from exposure to all those hot TV lights, but he shut it down cold when addressing juries. I'd done some sleuthing for him in the case of a police-siege-gone-wrong, but it hadn't worked out as well for his client as he'd hoped. Underdogs were his specialty, but he'd wound up exonerating the authorities, so he didn't like me any more than I liked him.

Philip Justice was his real name, and he swung it like an axe, in court and during press conferences. The founder of the family had represented Lucrezia Borgia or somebody like that, and the surname had been granted to him like a knighthood.

"You're sprung, Walker," Child said. "You kind of left this one out of your references."

"If I knew the lieutenant forgot to Mirandize you, I'd have saved a trip to the Frank Murphy Hall for a habeas." Justice's voice lacked the rusted barbed-wire edge he reserved for witnesses on the stand. "But he volunteered that information, so I don't see any reason to bring suit."

"I don't have a lawyer," I said.

Child said, "Duke it out between you outside. I only tanked you because it's good for my blood pressure. That wouldn't have been necessary if you'd told me you got Charlotte Sing in your sights. Now I can dust my hands of this one, Carl Fannon too, right into Washington's lap."

We adjourned to a sports bar in the next block, a cop hangout. You could cut the testosterone with a knife; and at least half of it was coming from female officers. A soccer game was playing on the big screen above the bar with the sound turned down. Not that anyone in the joint would listen any more than watch. A couple of talking heads were discussing the NFL drafts, with football season months away, and whoever was typing the closed-caption couldn't spell.

One lonely screen featured that day's Tigers game in Atlanta, taped earlier and abridged to cut out the boring parts; like whenever the Braves came to bat. A waitress wearing a Tigers jersey over a bandanna skirt brought us spicy chicken wings and a beer apiece.

"Let's tip twenty percent," I told Justice after she left. "She's the only one in here who knows what season it is."

"I have a box, if you ever want to see a game. I got a utility infielder off a date-rape beef and he's the grateful type."

He ate caveman style, one arm curled around his plate and looking up and around between bites. "We should've gone to my place in Southfield. Every time I come into one of these dumps I expect to get shot down fleeing arrest."

I said, "You can always bring suit from hell. You'll have your pick of representatives. I'm too busy doing Child's job to fight rush hour traffic. Who told him about Sing, you?"

"That'd be a violation of client confidentiality."

"How would tipping him off to an international fugitive get you in Dutch with Emil Haas?"

"Who said I'm representing him?"

"I left him calling his lawyer. Since guys like him don't normally truck with criminal attorneys, I figured his rep farmed it out to you."

He blinked more rapidly than usual. "We've never met. I've been retained by our mutual friend from Korea."

TWENTY-SIX

I dropped my napkin and stooped to pick it up. Not scrambling on my hands and knees out the fire exit was a test of character.

We kept our voices down. The blare from the one TV with its sound turned up and from a whooping party of fans next to our table drowned us out from all but each other. "Why isn't that a harboring rap?" I asked.

"Rule of law. Attorneys of record are immune. Also she hasn't been tried in an American court. Also she doesn't exist technically. The government in Pyongyang issued her death certificate. Our State Department could make a case overruling all that, but until it does I'm well in the clear."

"You're speaking in tongues, Counselor. If you implicated Sing in two murders, you violated privilege."

"I didn't do either. When I went to Thirteen Hundred and identified myself as your representative, Lieutenant Child was screening surveillance video from the entrance to the Annunciation shelter. He didn't throw me out, so I watched too. There's a dead spot between the last legitimate visitor and when you showed up, lasting about ten minutes. Now, who has the technology to wipe material from a DVD while it's being recorded, and from a distance?"

"Child worked that out all by himself?"

"Not just from that. You told him about Peaceable Shore, remember. You don't think he just let that drop, do you? The Detroit Police Department has access to the same high-tech equipment as Emil Haas. When Pacific Rim came up, and with it links to some of the multiple corporations it owned, including a Japanese manufacturer of electronic equipment, and then he figured out that anyone with that connection could use it to commit a crime—well, I'd shred a hunch like that in court, but there's no law against a cop keeping his nose to the ground until he roots up something solid.

"I kept my mouth shut," he went on. "You don't have inside information on an ongoing investigation connected to your client drop in your lap and blow it by bragging about the important people you represent."

"So why stand up for me?"

"Hear me out. She and I have never spoken or made direct contact. If I'm forced to divulge anything, I'd reveal the name of a legitimate venture capitalist in Grand Rapids who employed me to clear his technical expert of a hacking charge so he can advise him on how to protect his data from theft. I'm guessing he's never had contact with Sing either. Her whole organization is a Chinese box, politically incorrect as that sounds. I couldn't even swear under oath that I'm working on her behalf. Up till now everything's been hints and innuendo; which the rawest public defender in the system could prevent from being read into the record without getting up from his desk."

"How do you know it's her?"

He'd stopped blinking during his speech. Now he resumed. "Who says cops cornered the market on hunches?"

"Do you know our history?"

"Of course. You were something of a local celebrity when she made all the wire services."

"Did it ever occur to you she sent you to flush me out into the open?"

The sports fans next door let out another whoop and drank in unison. No one had scored; the rule seemed to be to take a shot every time the announcer told us what was actually happening in the game. At the current rate it would take them a week to work up a decent buzz.

Justice sent over a scowl and returned his attention to me. "Did I *say* Sing sent me?"

I waited. His habit of turning every conversation into a cross-examination was worse than the blinking.

With his condition he wasn't equipped to win a staring contest. "I've been summoned to a meeting," he said. "I hardly think she'll be present, but knowing what I do about her I'm more than a little leery. For all I know, one of my legal victories from before I knew she existed upset some scheme of hers, and if I go, I won't be coming back. Knowing what you know about her, I can't think of better security than to bring you along."

"I can. Don't go."

"That would be unethical. I'd already performed several services—which appeared innocuous enough at the time—before I found out who'd hired me. That makes me attorney of record. I could be disbarred for refusing to meet my client. What's funny?"

I stopped in mid-chuckle. "Now every lawyer joke I've ever heard makes sense. There isn't another species on earth that would choose death over forced retirement."

"And do what, write my memoirs? Don't waste money on a legal eagle's autobiography. The code of the profession demands he leave out the good parts. What else, join CNN? I'm too successful; you have to blow an open-and-shut case like O.J.'s to get an audition. I'd rather be dead. But just at the moment I'd rather be alive than dead."

"You don't need me to hold your hand. You must have a carry permit."

Automatically he slapped the left side of his suitcoat. The way it was cut, I hadn't been able to tell if he was armed. Some detective. Some tailor.

"Of course I have. In my game you measure your success in death threats. But I've never fired it except at paper targets, which rarely return fire."

"You don't want me. You want Wild Bill. The last time we crossed paths my weapon of choice was a wine bottle."

"You're the only one who ever got close enough to her to use it."

The TV announcer described a play. A member of the big party knocked back his glass, stuck his muzzle into a bowl of French onion soup, and made noises in it like an outboard motor. If you can't carry a load any bigger than that, you should give up sports.

Justice had picked up a wing. Now he put it down without biting into it and used his napkin on his fingers, one by one, the way a dowager takes off her gloves. He slid a gray-and-yellow leather case out of the inside pocket opposite the shoulder rig, uncapped a gold fountain pen, scribbled, tore loose a rectangle of paper, and glided it across the table facedown.

I left my wings on the plate, and my appetite with them. It had nothing to do with the guy playing Jacques Cousteau in his soup. I peeled up the hole card, peeked, and slid it back across the table.

"Too many zeroes. You trying to put me in a bigger bracket?"

Blink-blink-blink. "If you're seriously worried about that, order two more beers while I find an ATM."

"I haven't finished mine." I tapped the check. "You can hire a six-hitch team of professional bodyguards for that."

"Can I tell you a story? It won't take as long as my summations."

"Does it have a happy ending?"

"Depends on how you feel about Depression-era politics."

"I'm already laughing. Proceed, Counselor."

"In nineteen-thirty-five, an ear-nose-and-throat doctor with a grudge against Governor Huey Long of Louisiana stepped out from behind a pillar of the capitol building in Baton Rouge and plugged him. Long's bodyguard and a police officer returned fire, and kept firing when the doctor was on the floor. Hit him fifty-nine times, reloading whenever the cylinders clicked. Guess what the coroner found when he sliced the governor open."

"From what I've read, a liver the size of New Orleans."

"The thirty-eight slug that killed him. The doctor's gun was a twenty-five. Long could have survived that, but not a ricochet wound from a weapon fired by one of his own guards while they were chopping his assailant to pieces."

"I heard the same thing. I just wanted to hear how you told it. I also heard the bullet was from a forty-five, and that it didn't happen that way. The smaller caliber did the trick."

"Maybe so, but the principle is sound, based on the law of diminishing returns: Every time you hire an extra guard your risk increases fifty percent."

The waitress came, and went away quietly while we were staring at each other. He was getting better at it. I said, "All it takes is one."

"I did my homework. You don't lose your head in a tight situation."

"You're making me blush; but I'll pass."

"Scared?"

"Petrified. I've played enough poker to know when someone's trying to buy the pot. Cut it by two thirds and we'll do business."

"You're dickering in the wrong direction, Walker."

"Okay. Offer me three times as much. You got me out of custody and I'm grateful. Not that I was going stir-crazy after a couple of hours, but I can't do my job from the bucket. If I took that check, it'd make me so damn grateful I'd have to drop everything I'm doing and come running whenever you whistle. If that's what you want, you're going to have to cough up a lot more."

He drank and sat with his mouth full of beer. Then he swallowed, set down his glass, tore up the check, pocketed the pieces, and wrote another. An experienced lawyer can look daggers at you and write at the same time; but an experienced detective can read upside down. I took the check without looking at it and shook his hand.

"When and where? I need to stop and pick up my laundry." I patted my own left armpit; not that I ever wore anything as uncomfortable as a shoulder harness.

He traded the checkbook for a tablet as thick as a Pop-Tart and looked at the time. "One hour. Penthouse suite in the MGM Grand." He put it away with an expression like a pickled beet. "Must be a representative. Criminals only return to the scene of the crime in cheap fiction. Especially supercriminals who need to remain invisible."

I finished my beer and set the glass down in the center of the cocktail napkin. "How many supercriminals do you know, Counselor?"

TWENTY-SEVEN

t was a revolver job. I pack the German semiautomatic in the car just as a spare: That weapon lost two wars. The Zippo action required to expel a bullet is hell on accuracy, and I couldn't expect a smart schizo like Madam Sing to fall for that wine-bottle dodge a second time. I opened the door to my waiting room and looked at a wicker basket wrapped in cellophane dwarfing the coffee table where old magazines go to die, packed to the eyes with French cheese, Spanish peanuts, Dutch chocolates, and a bottle of Scotch that was old enough to run for president; a United Nations of slow but exquisite poison. A card was attached:

Bless you.

G.

Clipped to the card was a check made out in the amount of $1,500; my standard three-day retainer, making the twenty dollars in my wallet a bonus. Gwendolyn Haas tested as high on bookkeeping as she did on gratitude. Emil Haas had been cleared of suspicion in the death of his partner. I got that from the radio on the way there.

That figured. I'd earned the fee I'd gotten from Carl Fannon when I found Haas and why he'd disappeared, discharged my obligation there to Haas by speaking with him at the Liberty Inn, and given Gwendolyn satisfaction when her father ceased to be a suspect. If I'd followed my gut and refused the second check Philip Justice had given me, I'd be clear of the case. Who was I to trump all the authorities in Europe, Asia, and North America by putting myself right back in Charlotte Sing's sights?

It was the damnedest job yet. I'd never worked so hard for unemployment and failed so miserably.

There's some significance to the fact that the MGM Grand Casino and the traditional headquarters of the Detroit Police Department share the same address, 1300, on streets a few minutes apart. In both places the odds are with the house.

It's been many years since the last Wonder Bread truck rolled away from the site, but it's still a shock to the system to drive along the John Lodge Freeway without seeing its name spelled out backwards in iron letters on the roof. The dough made there now doesn't smell half as tasty or last half as long, and doesn't contribute a dime to the local economy: With a choice of lounges, nightclubs, and restaurants, four hundred guest rooms, poker rooms, craps rooms, slots lined up as deep as the Terracotta Army, and cigar bars gathered under one roof, the place is completely self-contained, a perpetual-motion profit machine, a city unto itself with its own police department and a population of three thousand employees mostly making minimum wage. The places spring up like weeds in our famous empty lots, choking out all other growth in the neighborhood. Every penny goes into armored trucks bound for Vegas.

I wouldn't be so sour about the racket if I hadn't lost ten bucks at blackjack twenty years ago and spent ten thousand trying to win it back.

From the outside, the building resembles the radiator of a showroom-quality Hudson Super Six, eighteen royal-blue floors with chrome trim on a concrete one-story base painted to resemble marble. The windows—like all the others in our town's public buildings—are bulletproof Plexiglas, and concrete White House–type barriers discourage smash-and-grab artists from driving stolen pickups through the doors, hitching up to an ATM, and dragging it home. Eight hundred million dollars on the hoof, and it had paid for itself in six months.

An electric sign mounted above the parking lot read:

WELCOME GEEK SQUAD

The lot was a sea of Volkswagen beetles painted to resemble police cars.

I went inside and got an immediate rush of piped-in oxygen, an old Atlantic City gimmick to keep the suckers awake enough to keep working the slots. There wasn't a Rat Pack member in that bunch: Someone had left open the door of the nursing home and the inmates were feeding in quarters from plastic cups, replenishing them from time to time from fanny packs and king-size handbags. You could smell the Bengay clear across the floor.

Practically everything there but the clientele had come from out of state, including half the staff. The antlers bolted to the ceiling of the Wolfgang Puck Grill are supposed to have come from northern Michigan, but there isn't that much venison in the Northwest Territory.

I climbed onto the stool next to where Philip Justice sat nursing a drink.

"I thought you'd never get here," he said. "Ten minutes listening to the jingle-jangle of those slots can give you tinnitus for a week."

The bartender was a polished-looking Pakistani in a green suede vest. I asked if he stocked Purple Gang.

"What's that?"

"They make it locally. There are only about a dozen breweries within walking distance of this spot."

"I'm sorry, sir. If your preference is a signature brand, we have a cellar full of imported beers." He uncovered a blinding set of teeth against dark skin. "Tour the world from the comfort of your bar stool."

"I haven't had my shots. Give me a Bud."

He stopped smiling and went to fetch it.

Justice had switched to a gin-and-tonic. "We're a little early. No sense looking too eager. You brought it?"

I nodded. I'd gotten tired of the slap-your-coat comedy and anyway the Chief's Special was riding my right kidney. "You?"

"Sure. Just a couple of gunslingers."

"Taking on the entire Sioux Nation in one ninety-pound package."

"You really think she'll be there in person?"

"I try to stay out of her head. I might not find my way back."

"I can't believe she's as bad as all that."

"Sure you do. It's why I'm here, swilling the King of Beers in a cushy whorehouse when I could be outside enjoying the kind of sunny afternoon we don't get often."

The bartender brought me an open bottle and a frosted mug, set each on a napkin of its own with the name of the joint embossed on it, and went to the other end of the bar to chase down a spill with his towel. I slid the mug out of the way and tipped up the bottle.

The place was beginning to fill with Best Buy techs dressed like Jerry Lewis: white short-sleeve dress shirts, narrow black neckties, and plastic pocket protectors. A couple of them were playing electronic poker at the other end of the bar, drinking appletinis and calculating the odds on trick wristwatches. It was Texas Hold 'Em. They were too young for tiddlywinks.

"How do we handle it?" Justice asked.

"Go in through the door. I've shinnied up enough drainpipes for one day."

"I don't mind telling you I'm scared shitless."

"And I'm not?" The Bud tasted like beer-flavored water. I parked it next to the mug, gestured to the Pakistani, and ordered Scotch neat.

"Yes, sir. Brand?"

"House label's okay."

"We don't have one."

"Dewar's, then."

He brought it in a thimble. I knocked it back cowboy style, asked for a double, and played with it. Justice watched me. "Don't you think you should keep a clear head?"

"It's okay. I coated my stomach with Old Smuggler on the way here."

"I just remembered why I don't like you. I never know when you're pulling my leg."

"You never heard anyone tell a joke at a wake?"

"And they call *me* a cynic."

"I'm not. I'm trying to put the butterflies to sleep. Got any notion what they want from you?"

"I was told it's a consultation. That could be anything from advice in a divorce action to a case for the Supreme Court. I got the word by e-mail same as always, from a server registered to the same subsidiary I traced back to Peaceable Shore. Except for meeting with the venture capitalist, it's my first face-to-face. Everything else was handled through the computer. My fee was direct-deposit." He spun his glass between his palms like a Boy Scout trying to start a campfire. "The message said it's informal, which I took to mean I should come alone."

"Uh-huh."

"You're not surprised?"

"I'd have been surprised if it didn't. I was wondering when you were going to get around to telling me."

"I was afraid you'd bow out."

"I still can, Counselor."

"If you do I go with you."

We drank for a while in peace, what there was of it with

a comic yelling jokes in the adjacent lounge over the racket from the one-armed bandits. The four-letter words didn't come back into his act until after the sun went down.

"I'll go in first and scope it out," I said. "Still got that tablet?"

He broke it loose. I found my toy phone and entered his number. "I'll text you the all-clear. One word: 'Brazos.'"

"What's it mean?"

"The Texas Rangers used to wire it to each other when they wanted to gather."

"Who told you that?"

"Hopalong Cassidy."

"Funny."

"It wasn't meant to be. We could use a little Hoppy right about now."

"What if it's not clear?"

"I won't need to text you that. I'll come out running."

TWENTY-EIGHT

The elevator to the penthouse floor was locked out to anyone not registered there. Justice's instructions were to pick up the key card at the desk. A compact blonde in a blazer looked at his driver's license and handed him an envelope with the hotel's logo on it. We entered a car with the same design in relief on bronze plate. The logo was repeated on the walls of the car, which was big enough to carry forty people without jostling. I leaned against the railing just to feel the bulk of the .38 in its belt clip.

Six weeks later the brass in Vegas installed metal detectors at the front entrance; I can't help feeling we were at least partially responsible for the decision.

He tried to slip the card in the slot next to 17 and came within about a foot of it on the first attempt; two on the second. He handed it to me without comment. I got it in without bending more than one corner on the first try.

We rose on a cushion of air. Except for a slight vibration I'd have thought we were standing still.

Justice was breathing as if he'd run around a country block. It reminded me I'd been holding my breath since we boarded. I let it out with a whoosh. The noise didn't make him jump any higher than the ceiling.

I grinned at him. "Everybody dies, Counselor."

"Have I said I don't like you?"

"Hurts just as much every time."

We ran out of conversation then. I leaned back against a brass rail and played with a pack of cigarettes. It kept my hands from shaking.

Up and up we went. I'd never traveled that far in an elevator without stopping to pick up more passengers.

At end of track we stepped out onto a red carpet runner deep enough to tickle our tonsils, with the MGM brand embroidered on it in gold every few feet. Bronze wall sconces lined the walls between doors, labeled the same. I figured I'd know the name of the place by the time we left.

If we left.

The door to 1700—at the end of the hall, meaning a corner suite—wasn't anything special, if you'd grown up in the Winter Palace. It was paneled in coffered mahogany, with its number scrolled on it in gold script. A pearl button was set back inside a brushed-gold socket next to the frame.

"What a layout," Justice said. "If just one of my clients slipped on a puddle of flop sweat in a gaming room, I might be able to stay up here for a month."

He was reverting to type. I felt a little better then. "Hero going in." I laid a finger against the button. The lawyer retreated a few steps and took up a position with his back to the wall and his hands folded at his waist. I pushed. A set of chimes played "Somewhere Over the Rainbow." I don't make these things up.

"Mr. Justice?" A male voice from the other side, with a mild urban accent; but then Madam Sing was an equal-opportunity employer, recruiting her squad of hit men from both sexes and every ethnic quarter. She'd have chosen this one to lull us into a sense of safety. I reached under my coattail and loosened the revolver in its cradle.

Justice cleared his throat and said, "Yes."

"Please come in."

I twisted the knob, filled my lungs, and swung open the door.

No one greeted me. No one shot at me, either; but the day was still young and there were plenty of places to hide.

It was a suite reserved for the occasional VIP from Washington or the Vatican, but more frequently for high-rollers, to entice them to stay long enough for the house to get even.

You could have moved my house inside that space without scratching the trim. The walls were a restful eggshell, hung with good reproductions in oil of old masters in gilt frames. A wind-torn scene of the destruction of the Spanish Armada took up most of the wall opposite the door, realistic enough to make you hang over the rail. Table and floor lamps bathed the room in soft glow, studded chairs and sofas invited the visitor to sink into glove leather. A liquid plasma TV the size of a bank mural was bolted to a wall, probably using railroad spikes. There were sprays of flowers and complimentary baskets, bowls of chocolates wrapped in gold foil, premium liquors behind beveled glass cabinet doors; and that was just the sitting room. The bedroom would have a swan-shaped gondola upholstered in hummingbird down and sprinkled with buds from an extinct variety of rose. Instead of a wake-up call, a gimmick attached to the telephone spritzed you with Chanel No. 5.

All Las Vegas, and all fake. The people who design penny arcades put more convincing veneers on diamond rings in claw machines. But it was impressive enough for Detroit, where anyone who drinks Schnapps from a glass is automatically an earl.

For all its gaud it felt like a place that had been abandoned for years. I let my arm fall. I'd been holding it bent, the .38 level, so long it had gone numb. The circulation came back tingling, like an electric current.

I spotted something I should have noticed before, a feature I didn't think came with the down payment on an overnight stay: A micro-tape player, doubtlessly noise-activated, on a table under the bright copper shotgun-barrel door chimes.

That accounted for the voice that had invited me in. I was alone in the suite, a place where my gun was useless.

I dove for the door; not quite in time to escape the incendiaries that turned the world into a ball of flame.

The back of my coat was burning. I followed through on the dive, propelled by the force of the explosion, belly-flopped to the hallway floor, and rolled, laying a black streak across the MGM logo for yards. I staggered to my feet, slapped out the last shred of flame, and leaned my shoulder against the wall. Down the hall, smoke poured out of 1700, around the door hanging by one hinge. I hadn't hit it that hard, although I'd tried; the blast had done the rest. Ahead of me the elevator door was closed. Philip Justice was on his way down, his mission completed.

I took the stairs, as we're instructed to do in case of fire. Here was where the glamour peeled off; the treads were plain brown rubber, the railing painted flat black, the lights ordinary fluorescents shedding watery illumination down the well.

I didn't hurry. I couldn't outrace the elevator, and just then the railing was my closest friend. I pulled myself along it until my ankles turned from Jell-O back to tendon and bone. Somebody was gasping; the sound echoed off the walls, painted a non-threatening taupe. The somebody was me, and he was still smoldering, filling the place with the stench of burning rags. I stripped out of the coat, let it fall, and stamped on the ashes until they lost their glow. I left it there and moved on.

The tan sole of a polished black shoe showed on the edge of the third landing as I came around the corner. A few more steps and there was a black lisle sock and a narrow patch of white skin showing between the top and a rucked-up cuff belonging to a pair of gray trousers. When you see a foot in that position it's almost never good news. I stopped descending, gripped the railing with both hands, and stood there waiting for my breathing and heart rate to slow down. When it was clear they wouldn't, I began moving again.

He lay on his back, as neatly as if he'd been caught beneath the arms and lowered gently to the floor, with one arm lying across his chest and the other angled slightly out from his body. His gray suitcoat was spread open, exposing yellow shirt. Light reflected off the button where it had come to rest on the landing after the thread broke. His hair, normally sleek as a seal's, was rumpled above the left temple, his head turned slightly to the right and one eye open. In death he was winking at me.

I accepted the challenge. I went down on one knee, not touching him. I'd made a New Year's resolution to quit stripping corpses or going through their pockets. If whatever had killed him didn't show itself in a cursory examination, someone else would have to handle that end.

Someone else got a break. Leaning close, I peered at what looked at first like a freckle just below and a little behind his left ear. Something had broken the skin, just a prick, slightly puckered and red around the edge. He might have been stung by a bee. He might have stuck himself with a shirt pin. He might have been bitten by a vampire with one fang. That was the likeliest of the three. You rarely hit the jugular purely by chance.

It hadn't been any of those, any more than a certain Bulgarian dissident had stumbled all by himself into the point of a toxic umbrella at the height of the Cold War.

They wouldn't have used that old gag; not on a high-profile lawyer who trailed death threats like Marley's chains. One glimpse at a bumbershoot and he'd have been a moving target, jeopardizing the operation. It would be more simple even than that: a Detroit-style mugging with a fatal ending.

I grasped the railing and pulled myself to my feet. I pantomimed the action, first taking Justice's part, then his killer's. That's what you do when you're a crack detective, play charades with the crime scene. He hadn't taken the elevator. Either he'd suspected it would be turned off in response to the explosion or someone else had rung for it below and he hadn't the iron will required to wait while it made its way back up. Encountering someone else in the stairwell, he'd have moved aside to let him pass. That was when he was grabbed, spun around, restrained with an arm across his throat—his shirt collar was rumpled, the knot of his gray necktie loose—and the needle or something similar injected in the artery. It would be a fast-acting poison, especially when introduced directly into the circulation. Ricin was trendy, the first choice of terrorists and would-be presidential assassins, but too slow. Unless someone had been monkeying around with it in a lab.

And who might that be?

TWENTY-NINE

I heard them coming from as far down as the sixth floor, clanging up the steps with their equipment rattling like a suit of armor falling down. The first one to the brass ring looked like all the rest in gas mask, oxygen tanks, and fireproof tuxedo. He stopped when he saw the body, almost causing a chain-reaction collision among the rest of the firefighting team.

"Smoke or burn?" The voice coming through the intercom built into his mask sounded like the window man at Wendy's.

"Poison."

"Repeat?"

"I'm guessing. How far behind are the cops?"

Child got up from his squat and sat down next to me on the bottom step of the second flight of stairs. "Next time I might just put on a HazMat outfit to talk to you. You spread murder like the clap."

"He came to me, Lieutenant. You were there."

The stairwell smelled even more lethal than before; the exhaust from the chemical spray the firefighters had used to quell a blaze of unknown origin made the air mustard-colored. The din of axes, thundering boots, and shouted warnings and directions from the top floor had begun to die down. There were no more sirens down below.

"Let's take it again." He jerked his chin at what I thought was the same uniform who'd opened the cell door at Homicide, a millennium ago. The officer flipped to a new page in his pad.

They took it again, as they had the first two times. I'd learned from long experience not to use all the same words, but not to plug in too many new ones. It still sounded rehearsed, but I was too tired to put that throb in my voice that says so much. They wouldn't have bought it in any case.

The lieutenant's first words upon recognizing the stiff were, "Well, hello, there, Counselor. We're gonna miss you between the auto ads and vaginal sprays.

"So you think the Sing character paid him to bait you into a fish-fry, then squiffed him to shut him up," he said to me.

"It's got a good beat and you can dance to it. It worked in the Fannon and Nelson kills. Why change now?"

"Why you? You didn't know anything more about what she's up to than we do. Assuming you didn't hold anything back. You wouldn't do that."

I waggled a finger in one ear. The roar was still there. "Sure I would. Not this time. That story Justice fed me could be true or part true or a load of compost."

"I never figured him for this kind of deal. Piss off a judge, always; suborn a jury, wouldn't surprise me. Accomplice to murder? That one goes down sideways."

"It did for me, or I'd have seen it coming when he sent me in alone. But if he performed for her once he'd do it again, accepting more and more by degrees. Once you step off the edge you don't start falling slower."

"Maybe we'll know something once the M.E. figures out what did the job." He shook his head. "I hate this cloak-and-dagger crap. Give me a good old-fashioned drive-by any day. I know where to start looking. Now come the G-boy toxicologists and then the band plays the Russian saber dance till they jerk the rabbit out of the hat. If you were getting close, this'd be the time to out with it. They make you behave in the federal box in Milan, not like our little bed-and-breakfast at the Third."

"I hit the wall before he came along. I'm thinking I was a side deal; repay me for that crippled hand as long as she was in the neighborhood."

"If she's only half as smart as everyone says she is, she'll let it lay now."

"Could be. If she were only half as insane as I know she is."

New light spilled down the stairs. An Adam-and-Eve EMS team carried a folding gurney with a zipper bag folded on top of it down to the landing.

"Guess they got the elevator going again," Child said. "Just when my BP got back to borderline."

"So take a pill."

"I do already. They say I need to eliminate some things from my diet. I'm thinking you for starters."

We stood to give the pair room. "Are we done?"

"We're done when you come down and sign a statement," Child said, "is my fondest hope."

I went back the way I'd come. The firefighters had finished destroying the door to 1700 and were chasing down scattered flames with short businesslike whooshes followed by the throat-tightening stench of carbon tetrachloride. Underneath was a metallic odor, somehow more evil.

"Magnesium and fulminate of mercury. Matches and gasoline aren't in it anymore; not at this level."

I looked at the mind reader. I almost didn't know him without his mask. Ray Charla wore his stiff fire-retardant coat and his helmet with its DPD insignia pushed back from his large parboiled forehead. He was leaning against the hallway wall with his arms folded and his metal toolbox on the floor at his feet, his tin mitts tucked under his belt.

I offered him my hand. "Amos Walker, Inspector. We met when Sister Delia's place burned down."

"If you say so." He took it as gently as he handled glowing pieces of evidence at the scene of a suspected arson. At that his grip would bend steel.

"You can tell what was used from the smell?"

He laid a permanently black-nailed finger alongside his nose. "For now, though I'll have to prove it with a chemical test before I put it in my report. I don't know how many more I've got coming. Sooner or later us burn guys blow out our olfactory organs. Makes us just as useless as one of those dope-sniffing dogs that get hooked. But not just yet."

"Who has access to magnesium and fulminate?"

"Not many. You need a license, which means a legitimate business that involves volatile material, and you leave behind a paper trail as long as the Miracle Mile. Still too many. Until the governor shut down that Hollywood incentives program, those special-effects boys went through the stuff like salt through a hired girl, as my old man used to say. There's always some leakage after a run like that."

I thanked him and left, making a note to ask Barry Stackpole if Peaceable Shore included any movie studios among its holdings.

Riding down in the elevator was a surreal experience. I couldn't help thinking about who had shared the trip up. I'd had no love for Philip Justice to begin with, and I tend to hold grudges against people who conspire to murder me; but the feeling was like facing the first morning after the death of someone close. As detectives went, I was about as hard-boiled as a thirty-second egg.

The police had evacuated the building, strung yellow tape, and set up barricades to hold back the crowd, shielding its eyes and pointing at smoke leaking from the blown-out windows in the corner room on the top floor. Film crews from all the local TV stations were pleading with the thin blue line erected behind the barricades; which in our city is pretty thick. They were as easy to argue with as the concrete barriers they resembled.

I inspected the Cutlass from headlights to rear bumper, in the event Sing had had some blasting material left over and decided to hedge her bet; but there were no unexplained wires visible from outside or under the hood, and when I crawled onto the floor of the front seat found no new options under the pedals and nothing more than a fat spider dozing in its web under the dash. I squashed it, using my handkerchief, and shook it out onto the asphalt. That made me feel almost as bad as I felt about Justice. It had probably been in residence long enough to be granted an easement.

The sun was waddling westward, scraping rooftops, while I let the wheel decide whether to turn toward the office or home. The office won; but that might have been the wheel misalignment I'd been putting off for a month.

Why'd I let the car make that decision? All my clients were either satisfied or dead. With Gwendolyn's money and what was left of Fannon's I could afford to take some time off. But I owed it to the customers who lined up outside the waiting room every day to lock that door and hang out the GONE FISHING sign.

At the first red light I got out the check Justice had given me, tore it in quarters, and stuffed the pieces among the butts in the ashtray. By the time the bank opened in the morning, the word would be out and all his assets frozen until Probate crawled from its snail's burrow to parse them out in order of importance. Which was okay with me. If spending the advance on a contract on your own life isn't considered bad luck, it ought to be.

In the shallow foyer, I took my ruined suitcoat off my arm and stuffed it into the bullet-shaped trash can. I didn't know why I'd bothered to carry it that far. Next to the can, the door to Rosecranz's narrow-gauged office/apartment was open, with his plumber's helper propped against it. That was for the cross-draft; he considered air-conditioning proof of western decadence. He existed without sleeping, working around the clock to keep the building from collapsing into the basement. He broke for a half-hour only, to eat and to shout answers to *Jeopardy* in Russian; I figured that way no one eavesdropping would know when he got one wrong. Sitting on a noisy rocking chair in front of a folding tray-table, he bellowed at his rabbit-ear set, slurping borscht from a bowl and drinking from a tumbler full of liquid too clear to be Detroit water. His back was to me, with the shoulder blades gnawing through bare skin. He wore only bib over-alls and woolen socks. After thirty years I knew everything about him except his first name.

When I got to the third floor the telephone was ringing in my office. That might have been going on for a while, with breaks in between. AT&T always interrupts to offer Repeat Dialing for a fee; otherwise it has to eat the expense of the bell. It stopped ringing, then started again. At the other end of the line was a patient and persistent finger. There was another pause before I could unlock the door marked PRIVATE, and then it started all over again. The little crack-ling silence was worse on my nerves than the ringing.

"A. Walker Investigations."

"How was your luck in the Grand?"

I'd been sweating ever since the stairwell where Philip Justice had died; now the perspiration wrapped me in a jacket of ice. A voice entirely without accent is an eerie thing. It wasn't atonal, like something generated by a computer, but the best dialogue coach in the world couldn't identify this one's origins either by continent or by nation or by re-gion. Its owner had spent nearly as much time and money on eradicating any such clue as she had building her for-tune in the international underworld.

"You know the answer to that," I said after a moment. "This isn't a recording."

"I'm relieved; truly I am. Don't you hate it when a worthy opponent fails too easily?"

"Not in this case." I barely heard myself. My heart was pounding in my ears.

"I have someone here who wants to talk to you."

The receiver creaked in my grip.

Another voice came on, shallow and rushed, as if the speaker had been running. "Mr. Walker, this is Gwen—"

Madam Sing took back the phone. "That should be sufficient. I don't want to insult your intelligence."

I leaned a hip against the desk. My own legs had given out. I asked the question for the second time that day. "When and where?"

"Have you seen your gift basket?"

My face felt hot suddenly. I set down the receiver, wobbled out into the waiting room, looked again at the card signed "G" attached to the basket; but then I hadn't had an example of her handwriting for comparison. I lifted the basket and examined it all over. Finally I turned it upside down. I read the sticker on the bottom:

GOODIES 4 U

A Product of Tranquility Coast

Suite 604

Sentinel Building

Detroit, Michigan

I set it down as carefully as if it were booby-trapped; which it may have been. At one time that had been all the rage in Korea, and she wasn't one to throw anything away just because its trend had passed; especially if there was death involved.

If I lived long enough, I might see the day when she exhausted all the synonyms for Pacific Rim.

If I lived long enough. I'd used up all my odds at the Grand.

THIRTY

ere I was, back where I'd started, an eon or two ago, and not in dog years. I felt like one of those plastic racehorses on a slotted oval track like they used to sell in the toy department at the five-and-dime. Only this horse was too broken down to get out of the gate.

The cops had taken away all the caution tape, leaving the Sentinel Building much as it had been when I'd first entered it, minus the surprise in the basement. The plastic canopy erected to shield pedestrians from falling masonry had acquired another coat of soot, and wind howling through the man-made canyon downtown had made a fresh deposit of waxed-cardboard cups, candy bar wrappers, crack capsules, and spent condoms on the pile inside the threshold of the padlocked front door, but that was an urban condition only a controlled demolition could reverse. I looked up at the ribbed façade and wondered all over again why they put ledges on tall buildings. Window-washers and sandblasters use scaffolds. Ledges are for suicides in search of an audience.

I went into the alley and looked around, but time hadn't gone backward and Frank Nelson wasn't there, showing off his tattoo and asking for money to buy frankfurters. I hadn't expected that; but hoping for the best is what keeps people off ledges. It's funny who the solitary life will make you miss. I was down to panhandlers and sleazy lawyers.

I'd thrown away the key Emil Haas had given me, but Madam Sing had overlooked nothing; the fire door wasn't locked. Once again I walked across the cardboard taped over the Pewabic, but this time I took the stairs up instead of down; even so just entering the well leading to the vault where Fannon had gasped out his life drew an arpeggio up my spine. Lately I'd been spending a lot of time on stairs, and they always led to something nasty.

She hadn't said to come alone, and I hadn't asked; we didn't want to insult each other's intelligence, after all. I'd have rung in the National Guard if she wouldn't stick a needle into Gwendolyn Haas at the first sight of a Sherman tank.

What did Gwendolyn Haas mean to me? We didn't even like each other. But one way or another I was responsible for three deaths on this case alone, if only because I'd entered the freeway late and had spent the time since accelerating desperately to keep up with the rest of the traffic. No matter how fast I drove, Sing had seen me coming and jammed down on the pedal, running over anyone who crossed her path. Her time as a slave had convinced her that life was as throwaway as a broken toaster.

There was no window to admit light between the walls that flanked the staircase. I leaned against one to fish out my flash. Something poked into my shoulder; a light switch.

The electricity had been on before, to power the laborers' halogens in the basement. I straightened and laid a finger on the switch, but snatched my hand away as if one of the wasps that still lived in the walls had stung it. In Arson/Murder 101 they teach you how to replace a regular switch with the arcing type, open the gas valves, and let the spark dispose of whoever turned on the light.

Sing seldom worked the same gag twice; but I'd bucked her system before. Even she wasn't crazy enough not to recognize when a rule has outlived its usefulness. I put on the flash, drew the Chief's Special, and started up, this time avoiding contact with the handrail. Poison was her new thing. She wasn't above coating the surface with a topical variety. She wasn't above anything you could name.

I prayed this was the finish, for more reasons than one. Another encounter with the gorgon and I'd be as paranoid as she was.

It took me most of a half hour to climb six floors. I stopped every few steps to hold my breath and listen. One of the advantages of stalking someone in an old building is it tells you who's moving around within earshot. One creak of a warped board and I'd shoot whoever belonged to the foot that caused it the moment he or she showed.

No creaks. In the silence I could hear horns honking several streets over, the whine and gulp of a heavy-duty transmission shifting up and down the scale and the huff of hydraulic brakes. I was as disconnected from all that life as an appendix suspended in a jar of formaldehyde.

I resumed climbing. I'd have traded those convenient stairs for the haul up the stuffy air shaft back at the Liberty Inn.

Rounding the fifth landing, I saw light and put away the flash. I leaned against the wall again, switched the revolver to my other hand, mopped my palm on my pants, then switched again and mopped the other. By then the butt was getting slippery again. I ascended the rest of the way crab-fashion, flattening my back to the wall with my gun arm stretched out along it. When I reached the top step I leapt the last six inches, pivoting right, then left on the bare wooden floor, gripping my weapon in both hands. An empty hallway yawned at me.

Either Detroit's plague of scrap rats hadn't made it up that far or the current owners had begun restoring the hardware. A series of fixtures shaped like women's breasts and paneled with mica shed orange light from the ceiling. A tarnished brass rectangle from the building's hotel incarnation directed me with arrows to Suites 600–620. I stood there with the .38, still in both hands, at my waist, for a minute. It was getting old, this business of waiting for my brain to catch up with my respiration.

Six-oh-four was near the end facing cross-town. It wasn't a corner suite. There was some comfort in that, until I reminded myself that Sing almost never repeated herself.

I knocked and struck the same pose, hugging the wall with my arm stretched along it, muzzle pointing at the middle of the door.

"Mr. Walker?"

That same male voice, a mix of Industrial North and Deep South.

"Uh-uh," I said. "Fooled me once. This time you open the door."

There was a silence while a drop of sweat crawled down my back, disguised as a fire ant. Then a latch grated in its socket. I pushed away from the wall, placed my right foot close to the threshold, and leaned my shoulder against the door. When it cracked open I shoved it with everything I had. The man with his hand on the knob stumbled backward, and was fighting for balance when I spun on the ball of my foot and swept my gun arm backhand, all the way from my left shoulder. I was Miguel Cabrera, swinging for the suburbs. The loaded cylinder—the heaviest part—caught him square on the right temple. He slung a thread of saliva across my shirt and went down hard enough to shake the building.

Standing in a crouch I eyeballed the room. We lacked two of a quorum, if that was where Sing was holding Gwendolyn, and all the doors were closed except the one I'd come in through. I slammed it with my heel, twisted the latch, and knelt to check the heap on the floor for a pulse. His eyes were all white as I pried back the lids. He was alive, and out like the cat.

He was a biggish black man, even-featured, with a shaved head that shone like a polished walnut bowl, a haze of gray lurking in the shadow under the skin. His right temple was bleeding blood, not brains, for all my effort. He wore a nylon jogging suit, blue with a broad white band that went diagonally from his left shoulder to his right hip and a narrower stripe down the outside seams of the pants. Air Jordans on his feet: white, new, and expensive. I patted him down, but I didn't expect to find a firearm. His weapon of choice was more sinister.

The right hand was partially closed. I pried open the fingers and looked at a slim glass hypodermic syringe. The naked needle glittered.

I'd sooner handle a live cobra in that condition. I looked around, found something shiny in the deep nap of the carpet, and carefully slid the glass cap over the point. I took the instrument out of his hand then, got up, carried it to a glass-topped table, and stashed it behind a bowl of cut flowers. If he came to while I was frisking the place, I'd have time to put him down again before he found it.

Neither the table nor the flowers nor the carpet made sense in a suite in a deserted skyscraper. The floor was cloaked wall-to-wall in snow-white lamb's-wool, giving off a chemical smell of fresh adhesive. Slim black-enamel floor lamps with umbrella-shaped metal shades made soft pools on its surface and the furniture was upholstered in pliant blue leather that lay back and begged you to make a running dive into it. What at first glance looked like pictures on the blue-and-silver-striped wallpaper shimmered and changed images: I blinked at Monet's water lilies, van Gogh's blazing haystacks, a Caravaggio, a Rembrandt, a couple of minor Picassos, and something that might have been a Klee; beyond ten feet, my eye for fine art needs a foghorn. It was some kind of trick holographic display on monitors in picture frames, wired to all the great art museums on six continents.

I didn't spend time admiring brushstrokes. I opened doors and stuck the gun into empty rooms: a mother-of-pearl bathroom with a sunken tub and rose-colored mirrors reflecting an aging and badly scared man, a master bedroom with a headboard six feet high with holes chewed in it by worms dead three hundred years, a closet I could park my car in, stocked with shoes too skimpy to be anything but Italian and clothing for every occasion and climate; all women's.

Small and slight as she is, Charlotte Sing couldn't have crawled into the toe of a Jimmy Choo. She'd given me the slip again; but why should I be any more special than the FBI, the CIA, Interpol, the French Sûreté, Scotland Yard, and the North Korean death squads?

And where was Gwendolyn Haas?

The last door was locked. It would connect to the room next door. Just to be sure I wouldn't be interrupted, I dragged up a Louis-the-Somethingth chair, tilted it, and jammed the back under the knob. The syringe was where I'd left it, the man in the jogging suit too. I picked up the syringe.

He stirred a little, winced, rolled his head to the side opposite the injured temple, and then his face went flat. His eyes flickered, but didn't open.

The revolver was superfluous now. I stuck it in its clip and thumbed the cap off the needle. I grinned at the shiny lethal point and squirted a thin arc of fast-acting poison to clear the barrel of air.

It was the first thing the man on the floor saw when he opened his eyes.

He got his elbows under him. I made a gesture with the needle and he stopped. He fixated on it. I could be any one of the heads on Mt. Rushmore for all he cared. The needle was the thing to watch.

"Where is she?" I asked.

His lips moved, but nothing came out. He licked them, cleared his throat, and said, "Who?"

"Mrs. Bigfoot, who else? Look at that." My hands were

shaking. It wasn't an act. "I'm getting old. Time was when you could blow me up, kill my client, a homeless innocent, and a lawyer, and I wouldn't twitch an eyelash. Tell me where she is—the hostage, too—or I'll find out just how quick this stuff works."

He said nothing; but his eyes slid toward the connecting door. They weren't standing out any farther than cue balls on brown felt.

THIRTY-ONE

wiggled the needle again. He lowered himself onto his back. I got up, scooted the chair away from the door, and rapped on the panel. After a week a metallic snap came from the other side. Considering whose fingers were on the latch, I changed hands on the needle and drew the .38; however fast the poison acted, a bullet was certain. I stood back from the door with it aimed at waist level.

The door opened. I let my breath out. I hadn't known I was holding it.

"How do you like my little pied-à-terre, Mr. Walker?"

Every time we met I was surprised by how tiny she was, barely five feet and built to scale. She could have bought her shoes in the toddler's department, if Nieman Marcus has one. The ones she wore were in keeping with those in the closet, black crocodile with red soles that showed when she lifted her feet from the carpet. She had on a black suit with slightly flared legs over a red heavy silk blouse with the collar spread over the lapels, showing a garnet the size of a wren's egg on a gold chain as fine as a spider's web; most appropriate.

She was hard on sixty, but could pass for forty—or thirty-six, if it was Last Call and you'd bombed out all around the cocktail lounge. A woman who could buy her way off the gallows could afford a troop of cosmetic surgeons as large as the North Korean Army. She had doll's features, and in her case "Asian" didn't quite apply. She was Oriental in the nineteenth-century use of the term, meaning enigmatic and devious.

The only unfashionable thing about her getup was the cast she wore on her right wrist, covering the hand almost to the fingertips, highly polished in red. The cast, aged dingy yellow, was the first I'd ever seen that had been in place that long without acquiring a single autograph. I couldn't think of anyone in the world who'd dare to come that close.

Apart from me. I'd smashed it with a wine bottle—the only weapon handy—badly enough to require years of micro-surgery.

At the time, she'd told me she was down to her last hundred million dollars. Those procedures, bribing a powerful Communist government, finding and preparing a ringer to take her place in the noose, explained her extensive investments in area real estate. Once she'd flipped it at a profit of several hundred percent, she'd be as rich as any oil emirate. With money like that she could buy a fleet of nuclear missiles large enough to turn the world into a half-moon, with her standing on the other side.

Not that she'd try anything so unsubtle. Her style ran more toward flooding the illegal narcotics market with lethal-grade heroin, financed by smuggling stolen human organs.

It all sounded loony enough for a Saturday morning superhero cartoon, and it seemed even less real that she was asking me if I approved of her flat downtown.

"Not bad," I said. "A little fancy for me. What becomes of all this when they knock the place down?"

"They meaning me. I intend to continue pumping cash into your broken city. Finding someone to take Carl Fannon's place is inconvenient, but he became a liability when he was clumsy enough to tip his hand to his partner."

"Speaking of Haas." I flicked my gaze over her head into the adjacent room. It was bare of furniture, fixtures, and imprisoned heiresses.

"Mr. Walker, this is Gwen—"

I almost dropped the gun and the needle. She'd turned her voice, a rich contralto with no regional inflections, into a Midwestern mezzo, an exact duplicate of Gwendolyn Haas's, right down to the breathless note on the phone.

She laughed that silvery tinkle that always reminded me of something scurrying inside a wall. "My voice coaches taught Hollywood how to sound like Londoners and cockneys to speak Alabama cornpone. One in particular had quit show business for a job in the White House, answering telephone calls in the voice of a busy president. I outbid his client. With what I paid those people to help me pronounce my *r*'s, don't you think I'd ask for something on the side?"

"Where is she?"

"I have no idea. Possibly celebrating her reunion with her father over dinner at the Blue Heron. I won't insult you with a windy story of how I managed to obtain a check with her name and address on it; anyone can get them from the bank, with no questions asked. Forging her signature was more challenging. She's right-handed." She held up the one with the cast on it. Just for an instant I saw a red flash in her eyes, which were so black they appeared to have no pupils; it was like the strobe of the coroner's wagon reflecting off the wall of a homicide scene. Along with being the sole person on the planet who'd gotten within striking distance of her, I'd scored another first: discovering she was capable of human emotion. Her hatred for me had grown like a cancer.

But then her every action was driven by hate. She was an Amerasian, ostensibly rescued from South Korea by her father, a veteran of the Police Conflict, only to be sold by him into slavery in a massage parlor back home, where a man with cash could get just about anything, even a massage. A thing like that can make a person practically un-American. Some people like to drown puppies; Charlotte Sing got her giggles chopping holes in the population of the United States.

"Even so," I said, "you went to a lot of bother just to take a swipe at me."

"Don't flatter yourself; it doesn't become that air of self-deprecation you cultivate so carefully. I employ people to run such mundane errands as a trip to the bank. I could have put any one of a number of skilled artists to duplicate Miss Haas's hand, but in this case it amused me to take a direct role. Which as it turned out was justified by that misstep in the casino. Had my current business taken me to New York or L.A. or Mexico City, I wouldn't have given you a thought. As long as I was here, making an example of you for the benefit of my more important adversaries seemed a good use of time."

"But not of money. A bullet would have done as well, without adding the Arson Squad to your list of adversaries."

"It was killing two birds with one stone. The prospect of the fire spreading throughout the building and causing the maximum number of casualties was appealing." She moved a fragile shoulder. "A juvenile mistake. I should have taken into account how much experience your fire department has had in extinguishing flames started by locals."

"You're slipping, Charlotte. Okay if I call you that? We've known each other so long."

"I prefer Madam. Translated in my native language, it's a sign of respect, but it has a western connotation I consider quite appropriate, given my past. I'd prefer it if you didn't smoke."

I'd juggled the needle into the hand holding the revolver—keeping enough distance between us to reverse positions—and plucked the pack from my shirt pocket. I tapped a cigarette out partway, speared it between my lips, struck a match from the book, and set it afire. I wasn't crass enough to blow smoke her way; I directed it toward the man who so far hadn't moved from the floor. I'd kept him nailed in the corner of my eye.

"I'd prefer it if you didn't slaughter people in case lots; but we've got the stars, we don't need the sun and the moon." I grinned. "I got that from *Now, Voyager*. You should watch it, take a break from *Dr. No*. What's the score now? Somewhere between Hurricane Katrina and Sadaam Hussein? Or am I being naïve? No one would miss Philip Justice except the lowlifes he represented, and the world can do with one less Fannon, but you could have bought off Frank Nelson for the price of a year's supply of Oscar Mayer."

"Frank Nelson?" A smooth ivory brow furrowed, against all odds: Industrial-grade concrete is pie dough compared to Botox. "Yes, the wastrel. Collateral damage. As loose ends go he was what your military calls an acceptable loss. The space he left has probably already been filled."

"How did you ever get anyone to stand in for you at your execution?"

"Conditioning, Mr. Walker. You'd call it brainwashing. Lord knows I'm a past master, having spent time at the other end. Promising funds enough to support her family for the rest of their natural lives is more of an incentive in her country than in most. I owe a great deal to tyrannical societies; they make any alternative an improvement, however horrific it may seem to yours."

"My God. You're worse than the people who made you what you are."

The shoulder lifted and fell again. Attempting to reason with insanity can crack your own hinges.

She stepped into the room, as casually as if two lethal weapons weren't trained on her. "What do you think of my artwork? All the great masters at my command, down to the last detail. Bill Gates, the master of our computer-driven society, commissioned it for his home, and I stole it out from under him, using much the same methods as he; in his case at the risk of a slap on the wrist from the Federal Trade Commission. At the touch of a button I can admire the genius of five centuries close up, right down to da Vinci's thumbprint on the *Mona Lisa*. He had a cut across it, by the way, possibly caused by careless use of a palette knife. Given ten more years, my scientists may be able to produce another da Vinci from the DNA in the blood he shed; a man who worked out the principle of flight by man, and who could draw a perfect circle freehand and perform exquisite calligraphy from right to left, so that his notebooks can be read only in a mirror? Am I so evil as to imagine such a thing?"

She was crazy, all right; but she managed to make perfect sense when she laid out her megalomania. That was the most dangerous thing about her.

She touched something under the edge of a table, and turned her face—that plastic, perfect face—toward a monitor in a picture frame mounted above a wet sink stocked with premium liquors. The Renaissance noblewoman pictured there, plastered to the throat in precious stones, flickered and vanished. The screen went blue, then burst into a stormy scene of a white horse twisting back upon itself in defense against a pile of brown sinew gnawing at its throat.

"Lion Attacking a Horse," she said. "George Stubbs, an overlooked master. It's one of my favorites. The head of the lion, you see, is hidden behind the neck of its prey; it could sport the male's ruff or the lack of it, which would indicate the female. In the wild, the male of the species bides its time, licking itself and preening its mane, while his mate provides the feast. The lioness is the hunter. The primitive world has understood that since the dawn of time. I owe my success to the failure of the modern world to do the same."

"Nice picture," I said. "I like Johnny Cash on black velvet."

Black eyes slid sideways. "I see you've deprived Mr. Bledsoe of his favorite toy. I warned him you wouldn't be as easy as Philip Justice."

"What's Mr. Bledsoe's story? He's imported, or I'd have

heard of him. We're strictly blue-collar here, shot-and-a-beer. No trendy stuff like wine coolers and ricin."

Her red-painted lips warped at the corners. She never showed teeth. It's an Asian thing. Park Avenue dress and good labials couldn't trump the conditioning of centuries.

"Ricin is a toy. In its standard form it takes days to work, and is traceable. My chemists genetically re-engineered the castor plants, crossing them with African frog venom, which conventional science claims is an incompatible combination, vegetable and animal, and bombarded the young beans with lasers. It took six growing seasons and many failures, like Edison's incandescent bulb, arriving at last at the colorless, odorless liquid you'll find in the barrel of that syringe. Be careful with it. A pint in a city reservoir would paralyze the population. One cc was enough to bring Mr. Justice's gaudy career to an abrupt end. Few will mourn. Every lawyer joke you've ever heard is based on fact, as far back as Shakespeare."

"That doesn't answer my question. Who's Bledsoe?"

Black eyes slid toward the man in the jogging suit, then back to me. "He's useful. The Detroit Lions offered him a contract, but he decided instead to have non-consensual sex with a concierge in the Hilton Garden Inn."

"Non-consensual my ass." Compared to our first conversation, this was a filibuster on Bledsoe's part.

"Enough." How she did it, without raising her voice, was no mystery considering her résumé; the one word cut him off like a razor across his throat. To me: "As I'm sure you're aware, today's professional athletes are no strangers to the needle. When I offered Mr. Bledsoe something better than minimum wage as a fitness trainer, he took less than twenty-four hours to accept. It's no nine-figure, three-year contract, but I consider it generous under the circumstances. Yes?" Again she looked at him.

"Yes, Madam Sing."

"Did Bledsoe kill Fannon and the man in the shelter?"

"Fannon. He was disappointed not to use his little toy, but it was important that Emil Haas be blamed for his partner's death. His word had to be discounted."

"And Frank?"

"The vagrant? That was mine. I wanted to test my street disguise and the portable wiping device I had developed in one of my laboratories; the same place that enabled me to penetrate Bill Gates's personal firewall."

"Like hell. Frank lived on a steady diet of protein, and you're just Tinker Bell's evil twin. He'd have broken you in half the second you picked up that pillow."

"I anticipated that, and borrowed Bledsoe's needle. I was loath to use it for the curiosity it would arouse at the autopsy. But it wasn't necessary. He stank of raw whiskey and was too far under to struggle." The doll's face creased. "If he was a friend, it might bring you comfort to assume he thought he was dreaming.

"I like to keep my hand in," she went on, "lest I get lazy and too dependent on my subordinates. I choose them for their ability, not necessarily for their intelligence."

That pricked Bledsoe's pride. He sprang up with the speed of a trained athlete and charged me, his bullet head aimed for my chest. I swung the .38 his way, stopping him in his tracks in the snow-white carpet. When I returned my attention to the worse threat, it leveled a shiny semi-automatic pistol at me and jerked the trigger.

THIRTY-TWO

The slug would be no bigger than a pencil eraser, but it was enough to drive me back two steps. I felt the wetness to the right just above my belt; the pain would come later.

She'd had the pistol hidden inside the cast on her arm. I hadn't thought about that.

I had a choice to make. Bledsoe was within striking distance and Sing had more cartridges in the magazine. The Chief's Special was in my right hand, Bledsoe's side. That made up my mind. I shot him and in the same instant swept my left arm in a sidearm pitch, letting the needle slip from between my fingers. It turned end-over-end twice and stuck deep in Sing's midsection an inch above where her suitcoat buttoned. It was good, and there was luck behind it, but I hadn't hit a vein. However fast the stuff worked she had time to shoot again. I shot from the hip. The little automatic fell from her hand and her knees gave out.

Another thud shook the floor: Bledsoe falling on his face, stiff as a cut tree. That's how little time had passed between shooting him and dealing his boss a lethal one-two. She made a lot less noise going down, folding almost gracefully onto her shoulder. Then, less picturesquely, she curled into a fetal position like a dying spider, her lips foaming at the corners.

Just in case all that madness and hatred still controlled her muscles, I stepped her way, kicked the pistol across the room, and put a foot on the cast on her arm.

The plaster cracked, showing a crevice of ivory skin. I didn't know at first just what was wrong about that.

I squatted and put my fingers against her throat. I'd sooner have touched an exposed wire; but there was nothing going on in the carotid. Then I took hold of the cast on both sides of the break and spread it, flaking plaster and tearing old gauze. I saw then what was missing. Human skin is always replacing itself, one layer peeling away to make room for the next. When any part of it has been confined only a fraction of the time as Sing's, the dead cells accumulate so that when the cast is removed the flesh looks like a laddered stocking. Hers was smooth, and nowhere near pale enough to have been veiled from the sun more than a few days.

A siren swooped a few blocks over. It had probably been going on for some time, but I'd been too preoccupied to notice. Someone had heard the shots and made the call; even in Detroit, people sometimes thought the noise unusual. I finished stripping off the cast, took the wrist between thumb and forefinger, and turned it this way and that, looking for the scars left by the jagged bones when they pierced the skin and the lacerations made by scalpels and lasers during numerous operations. It was unmarked. Charlotte Sing had the hands of a China doll, and this one had never been broken.

I felt dizzy. Blood seeped between the fingers of the hand holding my belly; but it wasn't entirely the loss of blood that had me reeling.

She'd done it again.

It wasn't the first time I'd been wheeled out of Detroit Receiving Hospital, but I still couldn't make any sense out of why all the bother, just to let me stand on my own two feet at the curb. I thanked the chatterbox of a nurse and hesitated before stepping up into the black SUV idling at the curb, an Escalade; a Cadillac in everything but style, comfort, and performance. You can slap a French label on a bottle of Thunderbird, but you can't make it champagne.

The door opened on the passenger's side and a youngish man in a black Polyester suit put a friendly expression on his pie-dough face. "Mr. Walker? Agent Craddock; NSA." He tipped open a leather folder containing something laminated with a gold seal.

"Thanks. I'll walk."

"It's four miles to your house. A man who's been shot—"

"My doctor told me I should take exercise. Who's your friend?"

The man behind the wheel, of similar vintage to his passenger, leaned his face across the other's chest. "Agent Winterhill, Homeland Security." Came out another set of credentials stamped in gold. "We've met."

"I remember." It had been on the other side of an anaesthetic fog in the recovery room, where they know how to deal with gunshot wounds from long experience.

"How are you feeling?"

"Educated. I've been suckered, shot, shackled, and set on fire. That last is new. I'll call for a cab, if it's all the same to you."

"You're entitled to counsel, of course; but you shouldn't need it. You're a witness, not a suspect."

"Either way I usually wind up in stir."

The cypher in the driver's seat made a quarter-turn. The sliding door behind the front seat whooshed open and Barry Stackpole gave me his barn-door grin. "You know they're hurting when they ring in the press for assurance. I'm going to give the introductions all over again: This gentleman is An Anonymous Source, and next to him A Source Who Asked Not to be Identified. Sorry if I've mixed you up," he told the two. "They turn all you guys on a lathe."

The young men's faces were as flat as playing cards. I shrugged and climbed in beside Barry.

I felt more comfortable then, not because of GM's attempt to stuff the seat of a glorified mud-dogger to feel like an Eldorado's. What he had on the spooks in front of us was between them and taxpayers. I hadn't made enough to file a return in three years.

"Okay if we drive around for a while?" Craddock asked. "Let us know if it gets to be too much. I can't imagine what it must be like to suffer a gunshot wound."

"I hope you never find out; and I don't even know you. Drive, Jeeves. Anything's better than four walls in ICU."

We rolled away from the curb. It felt like flying over Mount Kilimanjaro.

Barry shook out a Winston and held it across his chest. I

leaned over, nailed it, and let him fire it up from a throw-away lighter. My lungs took in smoke with a happy hello. "Et tu, Brute?" I said, blowing out a plume with the words.

"Relax, shamus. These boys are okay so far as spooks go. This whorehouse on wheels is a confessional. Nothing that takes place in it passes as far as the curb."

"That's what scares me."

"Amos." He leaned close, with as earnest an expression as I'd ever seen on that eternally youthful face. "It's you they're protecting. The more gaps you can fill between you and them, the sooner this thing goes into the file."

Winterhill, the driver, had fine hair, straw-colored and stirred by the slightest current of air in the car; he'd be bald in five years. He drove carefully, observing the speed limit and all the lights. I didn't trust him as far as the dashboard. "We know the woman you killed was an imposter," he said, "created by the late Madam Sing's organization in order to dupe the world into thinking she's still alive. These fanatics need a symbol, to put the fear of God into their enemies. We're still running the file on this one, the one you killed, but whether she took an active part in three murders is irrelevant. She was almost certainly an accomplice, either before or after the fact, which would make her death justifiable homicide. Same with the late unlamented Bledsoe, whose finger-prints you didn't quite manage to eradicate from the syringe he used to kill Philip Justice. Give us the benefit of what you've learned, and we'll wipe your slate clean. Do we have an understanding?"

I blew smoke. Current snatched it out the open window at my side. "Refresh my memory, please. We've got the FBI, the CIA, military intelligence, and the Cub Scouts. Why do we need you guys? It's like Ford and General Motors turn-ing out the same model."

Craddock belched delicately into a fist. "Nine-eleven changed everything, Walker. Everyone knows that."

"Do I? I've never been able to walk three blocks in any direction without tripping over a cop."

Something rustled. A thick manila envelope poked over the back of the front passenger's seat and landed on my lap.

I examined it from both sides, which were blank, ran my thumbnail under the flap, and pulled out a sheath of paper; paged to the end and looked at my signature in blue ball-point. It was my official statement to the Detroit Police Department. I'd signed it in the hospital.

"Stand by it still?" Craddock asked. "Nothing more came back to you after your head cleared?"

"No."

"Then consider it a souvenir. This case is closed, as far as local authorities are concerned. We've got it now."

"Slow down," I said. "What brought Carl Fannon to the basement in the Sentinel, when he was expected in Beijing?"

"We'll talk to Brita Palmerston, the office manager at Ve-locity Financing; when we locate her. You and Haas both told us he relied on her. He denies it, but we think he let something slip about wanting to meet you in the Sentinel, and she got word to Fannon. Maybe she was a double-agent, working both ends against the middle."

"I told Haas something like that," I said, "only I didn't say 'double agent.' Sounds like *Spy Kids*."

"Or she was a Peaceable Shore plant," said Winterhill.

Craddock said, "Anyway, we like her, and since she hasn't shown up for work or at her house in days, we're checking the airports, bus terminals, train stations, and car rental agencies. She'll fill in the blanks. For sure Fannon let his flight go and went straight to the Sentinel to ball up the meeting. We'll ask her who paid the freight.

"Charlotte Sing's dead," he said. "She's been dead since the North Koreans dropped her at the end of a rope. All this talk about a perfect double went to rest when you shot her in the Sentinel. We know now she worked in the Kyoto Spa near Metro Airport as a 'masseuse.'" He actually made air-quotes with his fingers. Trust a thirty-year-old virgin to do worldly. "The DNA checked."

"So did Sing's in Pyongyang." The cigarette had gone bitter. I powered down my window and snapped it into the slipstream. "You guys must use a corkscrew for a ruler. I can't wait to hear who killed Fannon, Frank, and Justice."

Winterhill said, "Bledsoe, of course. He had the build to manhandle Fannon into that vault and force a pillow onto Frank's face, and you caught him with a needle full of lethal dope. Your fake Sing took credit for Frank, on orders from the late Madam Sing's organization. As long as they can pretend she's alive, her reputation will continue to provide power. We know from recent history that you can't kill the terrorist octopus merely by cutting off its head. These people will travel on the gas left by their dead predecessors for as long as is necessary until they find another Madam Sing."

"That'll happen," I said. "About the time Christ comes back for His dry cleaning."

Winterhill stopped for a light. "Any one of those girls could win an acting Oscar. The better they are, the bigger the tip. She was as young as she looked, unlike her model—

not that either of them will get any older. And she was well-coached; by whom, we may never know, since you managed to eliminate the only two witnesses we might have asked."

"So sorry. Next time I'll bring along a choreographer."

The light changed and Winterhill pressed the accelerator. "Where to, Walker, home or office?"

"Office."

"All work and no play, eh?" Craddock looked smug.

"Screw that. I left the bottle at the office."

Barry got the story. He reported it on his streaming broadcast, copyrighting it first so the wire services had to credit him. Everything fit, the way he laid it out.

Which stank, and we both knew it. We had a theory about conspiracy theories: Life isn't a jigsaw puzzle. There are always pieces missing.

Over the smeared office glass on my desk, I got out the check the fake Charlotte Sing had signed with Gwendolyn Haas's name, tore it both ways, and dusted the pieces off my hands into the wastebasket. It was only the second time I'd destroyed a check made out to me, both on the same case. Knowing Sing, I thought it would clear, but the money would fester in my pocket. I had the satisfaction anyway of preventing her account from balancing.

Brita Palmerston cinched it for me. The feds never found her. Neither did her mother in Maryland, whom she'd called every day until the day I spoke with Brita at Velocity Financing. Missing Persons departments there and in Detroit—Deborah Stonesmith's detail—are still looking, along with every agency in Washington. They won't even find the body.

Of all the brilliant psychopaths with means, Sing's the only one so obsessed with detail.

She'd arranged for one double; why not two? Any street grifter can pocket the pea while he's switching the shells around under your nose. It takes a Madam Sing to put a pea under each shell and let you guess which one was the real deal. She's still out there, waiting, like a lioness in tall grass.